The Story Of Charles Strange

A Novel

Vol. I

by

Henry Wood

Double9 BOOKS

The Story Of Charles Strange
A Novel
Vol. I
by Henry Wood

ISBN: 978-93-71818-22-3

Published by

DOUBLE 9 BOOKS
2/13-B, Ansari Road
Daryaganj, New Delhi – 110002
info@double9books.com
www.double9books.com
Tel. 011-40042856

ABOUT THE AUTHOR

Ellen Wood, widely known under the name Mrs. Henry Wood, was a prolific English novelist born on January 17, 1814, in England. Her literary career gained widespread popularity in both Britain and abroad, especially after the publication of her most renowned work East Lynne in 1861. Her writing style combined elements of mystery, morality, and domestic life, contributing to her lasting appeal during the Victorian period. She married Henry Wood in 1836, and they had a son named Charles Wood. After her husband's death in 1866, she supported her family through her writing and editorial work. She also managed the magazine Argosy, to which she contributed both fiction and editorial commentary. Though many of her novels are lesser known today, her stories enjoyed international readership during her lifetime and were especially well-received in the United States and Australia. In Australia, her popularity once exceeded that of Charles Dickens. Ellen Wood died in London on February 10, 1887, at the age of 73 and was buried in Highgate Cemetery. Her parents were Thomas Price and Elizabeth Price.

CONTENTS

CHAPTER I
EARLY DAYS

I, CHARLES STRANGE, have called this my own story, and shall myself tell a portion of it to the reader; not all.

May was quickly passing. The drawing-room window of White Littleham Rectory stood open to the sunshine and the summer air: for the years of warm springs and long summers had not then left the land. The incumbent of the parish of White Littleham, in Hampshire, was the Reverend Eustace Strange. On a sofa, near the window, lay his wife, in her white dress and yellow silk shawl. A young and lovely lady, with a sweet countenance; her eyes the colour of blue-bells, her face growing more transparent day by day, her cheeks too often a fatal hectic; altogether looking so delicately fragile that the Rector must surely be blind not to suspect the truth. *She* suspected it. Nay, she no longer suspected; she knew. Perhaps it was that he would not do so.

"Charley!"

I sat at the end of the room in my little state chair, reading a new book of fairy tales that papa had given me that morning. He was as orthodox a divine as ever lived, but not strait-laced, and he liked children to read fairy tales. At the moment I was deep in a tale called "Finetta," about a young princess shut up in a high tower. To me it was enchanting.

"Yes, mamma."

"Come to me, dear."

Leaving the precious book behind me, I crossed the room to the sofa. My mother raised herself. Holding me to her with one hand, she pushed with the other the hair from my face and gazed into it. That my face was very much like hers, I knew. It had been said a hundred times in my hearing that I had her dark-blue eyes and her soft brown hair and her well-carved features.

"My pretty boy," she said caressingly, "I am so sorry! I fear you are disappointed. I think we might have had them. You were always promised a birthday party, you know, when you should be seven years old."

There had been some discussion about it. My mother thought the little boys and girls might come; but papa and Leah said, "No—it would fatigue her."

"I don't mind a bit, mamma," I answered. "I have my book, and it is so pretty. They can come next year, you know, when you are well again."

She sighed deeply. Getting up from the sofa, she took up two books that were on the stand behind her, and sat down again. Early in the spring some illness had seized her that I did not understand. She ought to have been well again by this time, but was not so. She left her room and came downstairs, and saw friends when they called: but instead of growing stronger she grew weaker.

"She was never robust, and it has been too much for her," I overheard Leah say to one of the other servants, in allusion to the illness.

"What if I should not be here at your next birthday, Charley?" she asked sadly, holding me to her side as she sat.

"But where should you be, mamma?"

"Well, my child, I think—sometimes I think—that by that time I may be in heaven."

I felt suddenly seized with a sort of shivering. I neither spoke nor cried; at seven years old many a child only imperfectly realizes the full meaning of anything like this. My eyes became misty.

"Don't cry, Charley. All that God does must be for the best, you know: and heaven is a better world than this."

"Oh, mamma, you must get well; you must!" I cried, words and tears bursting forth together. "Won't you come out, and grow strong in the sunshine? See how warm and bright it is! Look at the flowers in the grass!"

"Ay, dear; it is all very bright and warm and beautiful," she said, looking across the garden to the field beyond it. "The grass is growing long, and the buttercups and cowslips and blue-bells are all there. Soon they will be cut down and the field will be bare. Next year the grass and the flowers will spring up again, Charlie: but we, once we are taken, will spring up no more in this world: only in heaven."

"But don't you think you *will* get well, mamma? Can't you *try* to?"

"Well, dear—yes, I will try to do so. I *have* tried. I am trying every day, Charley, for I should not like to go away and leave my little boy."

With a long sigh, that it seemed to me I often heard from her now, she lay for a moment with her head on the back of the sofa and closed her eyes. Then she sat forward again, and took up one of the books.

"I meant to give you a little book to-day, Charley, as well as papa. Look, it is called 'Sintram.' A lady gave it me when I was twelve years old; and I have always liked it. You are too young to understand it yet, but you will do so later."

"Here's some poetry!" I cried, turning the leaves over. The pleasure of the gift had chased away my tears. Young minds are impressionable—and had she not just said she would try to get well?

"I will repeat it to you, Charley," she answered. "Listen."

"Repeat it?" I interrupted. "Do you know it by heart?—all?"

"Yes, all; every line of it.

"'When death is drawing near,
And thy heart sinks with fear,
And thy limbs fail,
Then raise thy hands and pray
To Him who cheers the way,
Through the dark vale.

"'See'st thou the eastern dawn?
Hear'st thou, in the red morn,
The angels' song?
Oh! lift thy drooping head,
Thou who in gloom and dread
Hast lain so long.

"'Death comes to set thee free;
Oh! meet him cheerily,
As thy true friend;
And all thy fears shall cease,
And in eternal peace
Thy penance end.'

You see, Charley, death comes not as a foe, but as a friend to those who have learnt to look for him, for he is sent by God," she continued in a loving voice as she smoothed back my hair with her gentle hand. "I want you to learn this bit of poetry by heart, and to say it sometimes to yourself in future years. And—and—should mamma have gone away, then it will be pleasant to you to remember that the angels' song came to cheer her—as I know it will come—when she was setting out on her journey. Oh! very pleasant! and the same song and the same angel will cheer your departure, my darling child, when the appointed hour for it shall come to you."

"Shall we *see* the angel?"

"Well—yes—with the eye of faith. And it is said that some good people have really seen him; have seen the radiant messenger who has come to take them to the eternal shores. You will learn it, Charley, won't you—and never forget it?"

"I'll learn it all, every verse; and I will never forget it, mamma."

"I am going to give you this book, also, Charley," she went on, bringing forward the other. "You—"

"Why, that's your Bible, mamma!"

"Yes, dear, it is my Bible; but I should like it to be yours. And I hope it will be as good a friend to you as it is now to me. I shall still use it myself, Charley, for a little while. You will lend it me, won't you? and later, it will be all your own."

"Shall you buy another for yourself, then?"

She did not answer. Her face was turned to the window; her yearning eyes were fixed in thought upon the blue sky; her hot hands were holding mine. In a moment, to my consternation, she bent her face upon mine and burst into a flood of tears. What I should have said or done, I know not; but at that moment my father came swiftly out of his study, into the room. He was a rather tall man with a pale, grave face, very much older than his wife.

"Do you chance to remember, Lucy, where that catalogue of books was put that came last week? I want—"

Thus far had he spoken, when he saw the state of things; both crying together. He broke off in vexation.

"How can you be so silly, Lucy—so imprudent! I will not have it. You don't allow yourself a chance to get well—giving way to these low spirits! What is the matter?"

"It is nothing," she replied, with another of those long sighs. "I was talking a little to Charley, and a fit of crying came on. It has not harmed me, Eustace."

"Charley, boy, I saw some fresh sweet violets down in the dingle this morning. Go you and pick some for mamma," he said. "Never mind your hat: it is as warm as midsummer."

I was ready for the dingle, which was only across the field, and to pick violets at any time, and I ran out. Leah Williams was coming in at the garden gate.

"Now, Master Charles! Where are you off to? And without your hat!"

"I'm going to the dingle, to get some fresh violets for mamma. Papa said my hat did not matter."

"Oh," said Leah, glancing doubtfully at the window. I glanced too. He had sat down on the sofa by mamma then, and was talking to her earnestly, his head bent. She had her handkerchief up to her face. Leah attacked me again.

"You've been crying, you naughty boy! Your eyes are wet still. What was that for?"

I did not say what: though I had much ado to keep the tears from falling. "Leah," I whispered, "do you think mamma will get well?"

"Bless the child!" she exclaimed, after a pause, during which she had looked again at the window and back at me. "Why, what's to hinder it?—with all this fine, beautiful warm weather! Don't you turn fanciful, Master Charley, there's a darling! And when you've picked the violets, you come to me; I'll find a slice of cake for you."

Leah had been with us about two years, as upper servant, attending upon mamma and me, and doing the sewing. She was between twenty and thirty then, an upright, superior young woman, kind in the main, though with rather a hard face, and faithful as the day. The other servants called her Mrs. Williams, for she had been married and was a widow. Not tall, she yet looked so, she was so remarkably thin. Her gray eyes were deep-set, her curls were black, and she had a high, fresh colour. Everyone, gentle and simple, wore curls at that time.

The violets were there in the dingle, sure enough; both blue and white. I picked a handful, ran in with them, and put them on my mother's lap. The Rector was sitting by her still, but he got up then.

"Oh, Charley, they are very sweet," she said with a smile—"very sweet and lovely. Thank you, my precious boy, my darling."

She kissed me a hundred times. She might have kissed me a hundred more, but papa drew me away.

"Do not tire yourself any more to-day, Lucy; it is not good for you. Charley, boy, you can take your fairy tales and show them to Leah."

The day of the funeral will never fade from my memory; and yet I can only recall some of its incidents. What impressed me most was that papa did not stand at the grave in his surplice reading the service, as I had seen him do at other funerals. Another clergyman was in his place, and he stood by me in silence, holding my hand. And he told me, after we returned home, that mamma was not herself in the cold dark grave, but a happy angel in heaven looking down upon me.

And so the time went on. Papa was more grave than of yore, and taught me my lessons daily. Leah indulged and scolded me alternately, often sang to me, for she had a clear voice, and when she was in a good humour would let me read "Sintram" and the fairy tales to her.

The interest of mamma's money—which was now mine—brought in three hundred a year. She had enjoyed it all; I was to have (or, rather, my father for me) just as much of it as the two trustees chose to allow, for it was strictly tied up in their hands. When I was twenty-four years of age—not before—the duties of the trustees would cease, and the whole sum, six thousand pounds, would come into my uncontrolled possession. One of the trustees was my mother's uncle, Mr. Serjeant Stillingfar; the other I did not know. Of course the reader will understand that I do not explain these matters from my knowledge at that time; but from what I learnt when I was older.

Nearly a year had gone by, and it was warm spring weather again. I sat in my brown-holland dress in the dingle amidst the wild flowers. A lot of cowslips lay about me; I had been picking the flowers from the stalks to make into a ball. The sunlight flickered through the trees, still in their tender green; the sky was blue and cloudless. My straw hat, with broad black ribbons, had fallen off; my white socks and shoes were stretched out before me. Fashion is always in extremes. Then it was the custom to dress a child simply up to quite an advanced age.

Why it should have been so, I know not; but while I sat, there came over me a sudden remembrance of the day when I had come to the dingle to pick those violets for mamma, and a rush of tears came on. Leah took good care of me, but she was not my mother. My father was good, and grave, and kind, but he did not give me the love that she had given. A mother's love would never be mine again, and I knew it; and in that moment was bitterly feeling it.

One end of the string was held between my teeth, the other end in my left hand, and my eyes were wet with tears. I strung the cowslips as well as I could. But it was not easy, and I made little progress.

"S'all I hold it for oo?"

Lifting my eyes in surprise—for I had thought the movement in the dingle was only Leah, coming to see after me—there stood the sweetest fairy of a child before me. The sleeves of her cotton frock and white pinafore were tied up with black ribbons; her face was delicately fair, her eyes were blue as the sky, and her light curls fell low on her pretty neck. My child heart went out to her with a bound, then and there.

"What oo trying for, 'ittle boy?"

"I was crying for mamma. She's gone away from me to heaven."

"S'all I tiss oo?"

And she put her little arms round my neck, without waiting for permission, and gave me a dozen kisses.

"Now we make the ball, 'ittle boy. S'all oo dive it to me?"

"Yes, I will give it to you. What is your name?"

"Baby. What is oors?"

"Charles. Do you—"

"You little toad of a monkey!—giving me this hunt! How came you to run away?"

The words were spoken by a tall, handsome boy, quite old compared with me, who had come dashing through the dingle. He caught up the child and began kissing her fondly. So the words were not meant to hurt her.

"It was oo ran away, Tom."

"But I ordered you to stop where I left you—and to sit still till I came back again. If you run away by yourself in the wood, you'll meet a great bear some day and he'll eat you up. Mind that, Miss Blanche. The mamsie is in a fine way; thinks you're lost, you silly little thing."

"Dat 'towslip ball for me, Tom."

Master Tom condescended to turn his attention upon me and the ball. I guessed now who they were: a family named Heriot, who had recently come to live at the pretty white cottage on the other side the copse. Tom was looking at me with his fine dark eyes.

"You are the parson's son, I take it, youngster. I saw you in the parson's pew on Sunday with an old woman."

"She is not an old woman," I said, jealous for Leah.

"A young one, then. What's your name?"

"Charles Strange."

"He dot no mamma, he try for her," put in the child. "Oo come to my mamma, ittle boy; she love oo and tiss oo."

"When I have made your ball."

"Oh, bother the ball!" put in Tom. "We can't wait for that: the mamsie's in a rare way already. You can come home with us if you like, youngster, and finish your ball afterwards."

Leaving the cowslips, I caught up my hat and we started, Tom carrying the child. I was a timid, sensitive little fellow, but took courage to ask him a question.

"Is your name Tom Heriot?"

"Well, yes, it *is* Tom Heriot—if it does you any good to know it. And this is Miss Blanche Heriot. And I wish you were a bit bigger and older; I'd make you my playfellow."

We were through the copse in a minute or two and in sight of the white cottage, over the field beyond it. Mrs. Heriot stood at the garden gate, looking out. She was a pretty little plump woman, with a soft voice, and wore a widow's cap. A servant in a check apron was with her, and knew me. Mrs. Heriot scolded Blanche for running away from Tom while she caressed her, and turned to smile at me.

"It is little Master Strange," I heard the maid say to her. "He lost his mother a year ago."

"Oh, poor little fellow!" sighed Mrs. Heriot, as she held me before her and kissed me twice. "What a nice little lad it is!—what lovely eyes! My dear, you can come here whenever you like, and play with Tom and Blanche."

Some few years before, this lady had married Colonel Heriot, a widower with one little boy—Thomas. After that, Blanche was born: so that she and Tom were, you see, only half-brother-and sister. When Blanche was two years old—she was three now—Colonel Heriot died, and Mrs. Heriot had come into the country to economize. She was not at all well off; had, indeed, little beyond what was allowed her with the two children: all their father's fortune had lapsed to them, and she had no control over it. Tom had more than Blanche, and was to be brought up for a soldier.

As we stood in a group outside the gate, papa came by. Seeing me, he naturally stopped, took off his hat to Mrs. Heriot, and spoke. That is how the acquaintanceship began, without formal introduction on either side. Taking the pretty little girl in his arms, he began talking to her: for he was very fond of children. Mrs. Heriot said something to him in a low, feeling tone about his wife's death.

"Yes," he sighed in answer, as he put down the child: "I shall never recover her loss. I live only in the hope of rejoining her there."

He glanced up at the blue sky: the pure, calm, peaceful canopy of heaven.

CHAPTER II
CHANGES

I SHALL never recover her loss. I live only in the hope of rejoining her there."

It has been said that the vows of lovers are ephemeral as characters written on the sand of the sea-shore. Surely may this also be said of the regrets mourners give to the departed! For time has a habit of soothing the deepest sorrow; and the remembrance which is piercing our hearts so poignantly to-day in a few short months will have lost its sting.

My father was quite sincere when speaking the above words: meant and believed them to the very letter. Yet before the spring and summer flowers had given place to those of autumn, he had taken unto himself another wife: Mrs. Heriot.

The first intimation of what was in contemplation came to me from Leah. I had offended her one day; done something wrong, or not done something right; and she fell upon me with a stern reproach, especially accusing me of ingratitude.

"After all my care of you, Master Charles—my anxiety and trouble to keep your clothes nice and make you good! What shall you do when I have gone away?"

"But you are not going away, Leah."

"I don't know that. We are to have changes here, it seems, and I'm not sure that they will suit me."

"What changes?" I asked.

She sat at the nursery window, which had the same aspect as the drawing-room below, darning my socks; I knelt on a chair, looking out. It was a rainy day, and the drops pattered thickly against the panes.

"Well, there's going to be—some company in the house," said Leah, taking her own time to answer me. "A *lot* of them. And I think perhaps there'll be no room for me."

"Oh, yes there will. Who is it, Leah?"

"I shouldn't wonder but it's those people over yonder," pointing her long darning-needle in the direction of the dingle.

"There's nothing there but mosses and trees, Leah. No people."

"There *is* a little farther off," nodded Leah. "There's Mrs. Heriot and her two children."

"Oh, do you say they are coming here!—do you mean it?" I cried in ecstasy. "Are they coming for a long visit, Leah?—to have breakfast here, and dine and sleep? Oh, how glad I am!"

"Ah!" groaned Leah; "perhaps you may be glad just at first; you are but a little shallow-sensed boy, Charley: but it may turn out for better, or it may turn out for worse."

To my intense astonishment, she dropped her work, burst into tears, and threw her hands up to her face. I felt very uncomfortable.

"What is it, Leah?"

"Well, it is that I'm a silly," she answered, looking up and drying her eyes. "I got thinking of the past, Master Charley, of your dear mamma, and all that. It *is* solitary for you here, and perhaps you'll be happier with some playfellows."

I went on staring at her.

"And look here, Master Charles, don't repeat what I've said; not to anybody, mind; or perhaps they won't come at all," concluded Leah, administering a slight shaking by way of enforcing her command.

There came a day—it was in that same week—when everything seemed to go wrong, as far as I was concerned. I had been at warfare with Leah in the morning, and was so inattentive (I suppose) at lessons in the afternoon that papa scolded me, and gave me an extra Latin exercise to do when they were over, and shut me up in the study until it was done. Then Leah refused jam for tea, which I wanted; saying that jam was meant for good boys, not for naughty ones. Altogether I was in anything but an enviable mood when I went out later into the garden. The most cruel item in the whole was that I could not see *I* had been to blame, but thought everyone else was. The sun had set behind the trees of the dingle in a red ball of fire as I climbed into my favourite seat—the fork of the pear-tree. Papa had gone to attend a vestry meeting; the little bell of the church was tinkling out, giving notice of the meeting to the parish.

Presently the bell ceased; solitary silence ensued both to eye and ear. The brightness of the atmosphere was giving place to the shades of approaching evening; the trees were putting on their melancholy. I have always thought—I always shall think—that nothing can be more depressing than the indescribable melancholy which trees in a solitary spot seem to put on after sunset. All people do not feel this; but to those who, like myself, see it, it brings a sensation of loneliness, nay, of *awe*, that is strangely painful.

"Ho-ho! So you are up there again, young Charley!"

The garden-gate had swung back to admit Tom Heriot. In hastening down from the tree—for he had a way of tormenting me when in it—I somehow lost my balance and fell on to the grass. Tom shrieked out with laughter, and made off again.

The fall was nothing—though my ankle ached; but at these untoward moments a little smart causes a great pain. It seemed to me that I was smarting all over, inside and out, mentally and bodily; and I sat down on the bench near the bed of shrubs, and burst into tears.

Sweet shrubs were they. Lavender and rosemary, old-man and sweet-briar, marjoram and lemon-thyme, musk and verbena; and others, no doubt. Mamma had had them all planted there. She would sit with me where I was now sitting alone, under the syringa trees, and revel in the perfume. In spring-time those sweet syringa blossoms would surround us; she loved their scent better than any other. Bitterly I cried, thinking of all this, and of her.

Again the gate opened, more gently this time, and Mrs. Heriot came in looking round. "Thomas," she called out—and then she saw me. "Charley, dear, has Tom been here? He ran away from me.—Why, my dear little boy, what is the matter?" For she had seen the tears falling.

They fell faster than ever at the question. She came up, sat down on the bench, and drew my face lovingly to her. I thought then—I think still—that Mrs. Heriot was one of the kindest, gentlest women that ever breathed. I don't believe she ever in her whole life said a sharp word to anyone.

Not liking to tell of my naughtiness—which I still attributed to others—or of the ignominious fall from the pear-tree, I sobbed forth something about mamma.

"If she had not gone away and left me alone," I said, "I should never have been unhappy, or—or cried. People were not cross with me when she was here."

"My darling, I know how lonely it is for you. Would you like me to come here and be your mamma?" she caressingly whispered.

"You could not be that," I dissented. "Mamma's up there."

Mrs. Heriot glanced up at the evening sky. "Yes, Charley, she is up there, with God; and she looks down, I feel sure, at you, and at what is being done for you. If I came home here I should try to take care of you as she would have done. And oh, my child, I should love you dearly."

"In her place?" I asked, feeling puzzled.

"In her place, Charley. *For her.*"

Tom burst in at the gate again. He began telling his stepmother of my fall as he danced a war-dance on the grass, and asked me how many of my legs and wings were broken.

They came to the Rectory: Mrs. Heriot—she was Mrs. Strange then—and Tom and Baby. After all, Leah did not leave. She grew reconciled to the new state of things in no time, and became as fond of the children as she was of me. As fond, at least, of Tom. I don't know that she ever cared heartily for Blanche: the little lady had a haughty face, and sometimes a haughty way with her.

We were all as happy as the day was long. Mrs. Strange indulged us all. Tom was a dreadful pickle—it was what the servants called him; but they all adored him. He was a handsome, generous, reckless boy, two years older than myself in years, twice two in height and advancement. He teased Leah's life out of her; but the more he teased, the better she liked him. He teased Blanche, he teased me; though he would have gone through fire and water for either of us, ay, and laid down his life any moment to save ours. He was everlastingly in mischief indoors or out. He called papa "sir" to his face, "the parson" or "his reverence" behind his back. There was no taming Tom Heriot.

For a short time papa took Tom's lessons with mine. But he found it would not answer. Tom's guardians wrote to beg of the Rector to continue to undertake him for a year or two, offering a handsome recompense in return. But my father wrote word back that the lad needed the discipline of school and must have it. So to school Tom was sent. He came home in the holidays, reckless and random, generous and loving as ever, and we had fine times together, the three of us growing up like brothers and sister. Of course, I was not related to them at all: and they were only half related to each other.

Rather singularly, Thomas Heriot's fortune was just as much as mine: six thousand pounds: and left in very much the same way. The interest, three hundred a year, was to maintain and educate him for the army; and he would come into the whole when he was twenty-one. Blanche had less: four thousand pounds only, and it was secured in the same way as Tom's was until she should be twenty-one, or until she married.

And thus about a couple of years went on.

No household was ever less given to superstition than ours at White Littleham Rectory. It never as much as entered the mind of any of its inmates, from its master downwards. And perhaps it was this complete indifference to and disbelief in the supernatural that caused the matter to be openly spoken of by the Rector. I have since thought so.

It was Christmas-tide, and Christmas weather. Frost and snow covered the ground. Icicles on the branches glittered in the sunshine like diamonds.

"It is the jolliest day!" exclaimed Tom, dashing into the breakfast-room from an early morning run half over the parish. "People are slipping about like mad, and the ice is inches thick on the ponds. Old Joe Styles went right down on his back."

"I hope he was not hurt, Tom," remarked papa, coming down from his chamber into the room in time to hear the last sentence. "Good-morning, my boys."

"Oh, it was only a Christmas gambol, sir," said Tom carelessly.

We sat down to breakfast. Leah came in to see to me and Tom. The Rector might be—and was—efficient in his parish and pulpit, but a more hopelessly incapable man in a domestic point of view the world never saw. Tom and I should have come badly off had we relied upon him to help us, and we might have gobbled up every earthly thing on the table without his saying yea or nay. Leah, knowing this, stood to pour out the coffee. Mrs. Strange had gone away to London on Wednesday (the day after Christmas Day) to see an old aunt who was ill, and had taken Blanche with her. This was Friday, and they were expected home again on the morrow.

Presently Tom, who was observant in his way, remarked that papa was taking nothing. His coffee stood before him untouched; some bacon lay neglected on his plate.

"Shall I cut you some thin bread and butter, sir?" asked Leah.

"Presently," said he, and went on doing nothing as before.

"What are you thinking of, papa?"

"Well, Charley, I—I was thinking of my dream," he answered. "I suppose it *was* a dream," he went on, as if to himself. "But it was a curious one."

"Oh, please tell it us!" I cried. "I dreamt on Christmas night that I had a splendid plum-cake, and was cutting it up into slices."

"Well—it was towards morning," he said, still speaking in a dreamy sort of way, his eyes looking straight out before him as if he were recalling it, yet evidently seeing nothing. "I awoke suddenly with the sound of a voice in my ear. It was your mamma's voice, Charley; your own mother's; and she seemed to be standing at my bedside. 'I am coming for you,' she said to me—or seemed to say. I was wide awake in a moment, and knew her voice perfectly. Curious, was it not, Leah?"

Leah, cutting bread and butter for Tom, had halted, loaf in one hand, knife in the other.

"Yes, sir," she answered, gazing at the Rector. "Did you *see* anything, sir?"

"No; not exactly," he returned. "I was conscious that whoever spoke to me, stood close to my bedside; and I was also conscious that the figure retreated across the room towards the window. I cannot say that I absolutely saw the movement; it was more like some unseen presence in the room. It was very odd. Somehow I can't get it out of my head— Why, here's Mr. Penthorn!" he broke off to say.

Mr. Penthorn had opened the gate, and was walking briskly up the path. He was our doctor; a gray-haired man, active and lively, and very friendly with us all. He had looked in, in passing back to the village, to tell the Rector that a parishioner, to whom he had been called up in the night, was in danger.

"I'll go and see her," said papa. "You'd be none the worse for a cup of coffee, Penthorn. It is sharp weather."

"Well, perhaps I shouldn't," said he, sitting down by me, while Tom went off to the kitchen for a cup and saucer. "Sharp enough—but seasonable. Is anything amiss with you, Leah? Indigestion again?"

This caused us to look at Leah. She was whiter than the table-cloth.

"No, sir; I'm all right," answered Leah, as she took the cup from Tom's hand and began to fill it with coffee and hot milk. "Something that the master has been telling us scared me a bit at the moment, that's all."

"And what was that?" asked the Doctor lightly.

So the story had to be gone over again, papa repeating it rather more elaborately. Mr. Penthorn was sceptical, and said it was a dream.

"I have just called it a dream," assented my father. "But, in one sense, it was certainly not a dream. I had not been dreaming at all, to my knowledge; have not the least recollection of doing so. I woke up fully in a moment, with the voice ringing in my ears."

"The voice must have been pure fancy," declared Mr. Penthorn.

"That it certainly was not," said the Rector. "I never heard a voice more plainly in my life; every tone, every word was distinct and clear. No, Penthorn; that someone spoke to me is certain; the puzzle is—who was it?"

"Someone must have got into your room, then," said the Doctor, throwing his eyes suspiciously across the table at Tom.

Leah turned sharply round to face Tom. "Master Tom, if you played this trick, say so," she cried, her voice trembling.

"I! that's good!" retorted Tom, as earnestly as he could speak. "I never got out of bed from the time I got into it. Wasn't likely to. I never woke up at all."

"It was not Tom," interposed papa. "How could Tom assume my late wife's voice? It *was* her voice, Penthorn. I had never heard it since she left us; and it has brought back all its familiar tones to my memory."

The Doctor helped himself to some bread and butter, and gave his head a shake.

"Besides," resumed the Rector, "no one else ever addressed me as she did—'Eustace.' I have not been called Eustace since my mother died, many years ago, except by her. My present wife has never called me by it."

That was true. Mrs. Strange had a pet name for him, and it was "Hubby."

"'I am coming for you, Eustace,' said the voice. It was her voice; her way of speaking. I can't account for it at all, Penthorn. I can't get it out of my head, though it sounds altogether so ridiculous."

"Well, I give it up," said Mr. Penthorn, finishing his coffee. "If you *were* awake, Strange, someone must have been essaying a little sleight-of-hand upon you. Good-morning, all of you; I must be off to my patients. Tom Heriot, don't you get trying the ponds yet, or maybe I shall have you on my hands as well as other people."

We gave it up also: and nothing more was said or thought of it, as far as I know. We were not, I repeat, a superstitious family. Papa went about his duties as usual, and Leah went about hers. The next day, Saturday, Mrs.

Strange and Blanche returned home; and the cold grew sharper and the frozen ponds were lovely.

On Monday afternoon, the last day of the year, the Rector mounted old Dobbin, to ride to the next parish. He had to take a funeral for the incumbent, who was in bed with gout.

"Have his shoes been roughed?" asked Tom, standing at the gate with me to watch the start.

"Yes; and well roughed too, Master Tom," spoke up James, who had lived with us longer than I could remember, as gardener, groom, and general man-of-all-work. "'Tisn't weather, sir, to send him out without being rough-shod."

"You two boys had better get to your Latin for an hour, and prepare it for me for to-morrow; and afterwards you may go to the ponds," said my father, as he rode away. "Good-bye, lads. Take care of yourself, Charley."

"Bother Latin!" said Tom. "I'm going off now. Will you come, youngster?"

"Not till I've done my Latin."

"You senseless young donkey! Stay, though; I must tell the mamsie something."

He made for the dining-room, where Mrs. Strange sat with Blanche. "Look here, mamsie," said he; "let us have a bit of a party to-night."

"A party, Tom!" she returned.

"Just the young Penthorns and the Clints."

"Oh, do, mamma!" I cried, for I was uncommonly fond of parties. And "Do, mamma!" struck in little Blanche.

My new mother rarely denied us anything; but she hesitated now.

"I think not to-night, dears. You know we are going to have the school-treat tomorrow evening, and the servants are busy with the cakes and things. They shall come on Wednesday instead, Tom."

Tom laughed. "They *must* come to-night, mamsie. They *are* coming. I have asked them."

"What—the young Penthorns?"

"*And* the young Clints," said Tom, clasping his stepmother, and kissing her. "They'll be here on the stroke of five. Mind you treat us to plenty of tarts and cakes, there's a good mamsie!"

Tom went off with his skates. I got to my books. After that, some friends came to call, and the afternoon seemed to pass in no time.

"It is hardly worth while your going to the ponds now, Master Charles," said Leah, meeting me in the passage, when I was at last at liberty.

In looking back I think that I must have had a very obedient nature, for I was ever willing to listen to orders or suggestions, however unpalatable they might be. Passing through the back-door, the nearest way to the square pond, to which Tom had gone, I looked out. Twilight was already setting in. The evening star twinkled in a clear, frosty sky. The moon shone like a silver shield.

"Before you could get to the square pond, Master Charley, it would be dark," said Leah, as she stood beside me.

"So it would," I assented. "I think I'll not go, Leah."

"And I'm sure you don't need to tire yourself for to-night," went on Leah. "There'll be romping enough and to spare if those boys and girls come."

I went back to the parlour. Leah walked to the side gate, wondering (as she said afterwards) what had come to the milkman, for he was generally much earlier. As she stood looking down the lane, she saw Tom stealing up.

"He has been in some mischief," decided Leah. "It's not like *him* to creep up in that timorous fashion. Good patience! Why, the lad must have had a fright; his face is white as death."

"Leah!" said the boy, shrinking as he glanced over his shoulder. "Leah!"

"Well, what on earth is it?" asked Leah, feeling a little dread herself. "What have you been up to at that pond? You've not been in it yourself, I suppose!"

"Papa—the parson—is lying in the road by the triangle, all pale and still. He does not move."

Whenever Master Tom Heriot saw a chance of scaring the kitchen with a fable, he plunged into one. Leah peered at him doubtfully in the fading light.

"I think he is dead. I'm sure he is," continued Tom, bursting into tears.

This convinced Leah. She uttered a faint cry.

"We took that way back from the square pond; I, and Joe and Bertie Penthorn. They were going home to get ready to come here. Then we saw something lying near the triangle, close to that heap of flint-stones. It was *him*, Leah. Oh! what is to be done? I can't tell mamma, or poor Charley."

James ran up, all scared, as Tom finished speaking. He had found Dobbin at the stable-door, without sign or token of his master.

Even yet I cannot bear to think of that dreadful night. We *had* to be told, you see; and Leah lost no time over it. While Tom came home with the news, Joe Penthorn had run for his father, and Bertie called to some labourers who were passing on the other side of the triangle.

He was brought home on a litter, the men carrying it, Mr. Penthorn walking by its side. He was not dead, but quite unconscious. They put a mattress on the study-table, and laid him on it.

He had been riding home from the funeral. Whether Dobbin, usually so sure-footed and steady, had plunged his foot into a rut, just glazed over by the ice, and so had stumbled; or whether something had startled him and caused him to swerve, we never knew. The Rector had been thrown violently, his head striking the stones.

Mr. Penthorn did not leave the study. Two other surgeons, summoned in haste from the neighbouring town, joined him. They could do nothing for papa—*nothing*. He never recovered consciousness, and died during the night—about a quarter before three o'clock.

"I knew he would go just at this time, sir," whispered Leah to Mr. Penthorn as he was leaving the house and she opened the front-door for him. "I felt sure of it when the doctors said he would not see morning light. It was just at the same hour that he had his call, sir, three nights ago. As sure as that he is now lying there dead, as sure as that those stars are shining in the heavens above us, *that was his warning*."

"Nonsense, Leah!" reproved Mr. Penthorn sharply.

Chances and changes. The world is full of them. A short time and White Littleham Rectory knew us no more. The Reverend Eustace Strange was sleeping his last sleep in the churchyard by his wife's side, and the Reverend John Ravensworth was the new Rector.

Tom Heriot went back to school. I was placed at one chosen for me by my great-uncle, Mr. Serjeant Stillingfar. Leah Williams left us to take service in another family, who were about to settle somewhere on the Continent. She could not speak for emotion when she said good-bye to me.

"It must be for years, Master Charles, and it may be for ever," she said, taking, I fancy, the words from one of the many favourite ditties, martial or love-lorn, she treated us to in the nursery. "No, we may never meet again in this life, Master Charles. All the same, I hope we shall."

And meet we did, though not for years and years. And it would no doubt have called forth indignation from Leah had I been able to foretell how, when that meeting came in after-life, she would purposely withhold her identity from me and pass herself off as a stranger.

Mrs. Strange went to London, Blanche with her, to take up for the present her abode with her old aunt, who had invited her to do so. She was little, if any, better off in this second widowhood than she had been as the widow of Colonel Heriot. What papa had to leave he left to her; but it was not much. I had my own mother's money. And so we were all separated again; all divided: one here, another there, a third elsewhere. It is the way of the world. Change and chance! chance and change!

CHAPTER III
MR. SERJEANT STILLINGFAR

Gloucester Place, Portman Square. In one of its handsome houses—as they are considered to be by persons of moderate desires—dwelt its owner, Major Carlen. Major Carlen was a man of the world; a man of fashion. When the house had fallen to him some years before by the will of a relative, with a substantial sum of money to keep it up, he professed to despise the house to his brother-officers and other acquaintances of the great world. He would have preferred a house in Belgrave Square, or in Grosvenor Place, or in Park Lane. Major Carlen was accustomed to speak largely; it was his way.

Since then, he had retired from the army, and was master of himself, his time and his amusements. Major Carlen was fond of clubs, fond of card-playing, fond of dinners; fond, indeed, of whatever constitutes fast life. His house in Gloucester Place was handsomely furnished, replete with comfort, and possessed every reasonable requisite for social happiness—even to a wife. And Major Carlen's wife was Jessy, once Mrs. Strange, once Mrs. Heriot.

It is quite a problem why some women cannot marry at all, try to do so as they may, whilst others become wives three and four times over, and without much seeking of their own. Mrs. Heriot (to give her her first name) was one of these. In very little more than a year after her first husband died, she married her second; in not any more than a year after her second husband's death, she married her third. Major Carlen must have been captivated by her pretty face and purring manner; whilst she fell prone at the feet of the man of fashion, and perhaps a very little at the prospect of being mistress of the house in Gloucester Place. Anyway, the why and the wherefore lay between themselves. Mrs. Strange became Mrs. Carlen.

Reading over thus far, it has struck me that you may reasonably think the story is to consist chiefly of marrying and dying; for there has been an undue proportion of both events. Not so: as you will find as you go on. Our ancestors do marry and die, you know: and these first three chapters are only a prologue to the story which has to come.

Christmas has come round again. Not the Christmas following that which ended so disastrously for us at White Littleham Rectory, but one five years later. For the stream of time flows on its course, and boys and girls grow insensibly towards men and women.

It had been a green Christmas this year. We were now some days past it. The air was mild, the skies were blue and genial. Newspapers told of violets and other flowers growing in nooks, sheltered and unsheltered. Mrs. Carlen, seated by a well-spread table, half dinner, half tea, in the dining-room at Gloucester Place, declared that the fire made the room too warm. I was reading. Blanche, a very fair and pretty girl, now ten years old, sat on a stool on the hearthrug, her light curls tied back with blue ribbons, her hands lying idly on the lap of her short silk frock. We were awaiting an arrival.

"Listen, Charles!" cried mamma—as I called her still. "I do think a cab is stopping."

I put down my book, and Blanche threw back her head and her blue ribbons in expectation. But the cab went on.

"It is just like Tom!" smiled Mrs. Carlen. "Nothing ever put him out as it does other people. He gives us one hour and means another. He *said* seven o'clock, so we may expect him at ten. I do wish he could have obtained leave for Christmas Day!"

Major Carlen did not like children, boys especially: yet Tom Heriot and I had been allowed to spend our holidays at his house, summer and winter. Mrs. Carlen stood partly in the light of a mother to us both; and I expect our guardians paid substantially for the privilege. Tom was now nearly eighteen, and had had a commission given him in a crack regiment; partly, it was said, through the interest of Major Carlen. I was between fifteen and sixteen.

"I'm sure you children must be famishing," cried Mrs. Carlen. "It wants five minutes to eight. If Tom is not here as the clock strikes, we will begin tea."

The silvery bell had told its eight strokes and was dying away, when a cab dashing past the door suddenly pulled up. No mistake this time. We heard Tom's voice abusing the driver—or, as he called it, "pitching into him"—for not looking at the numbers.

What a fine, handsome young fellow he had grown! And how joyously he met us all; folding mother, brother and sister in one eager embrace. Tom Heriot was careless and thoughtless as it was possible for anyone to be, but he had a warm and affectionate heart. When trouble, and something worse, fell upon him later, and he became a town's talk, people called him bad-hearted amongst other reproaches; but they were mistaken.

"Why, Charley, how you have shot up!" he cried gaily. "You'll soon overtake me."

I shook my head. "While I am growing, Tom, you will be growing also."

"What was it you said in your last letter?" he went on, as we began tea. "That you were going to leave school?"

"Well, I fancy so, Tom. Uncle Stillingfar gave notice at Michaelmas."

"Thinks you know enough, eh, lad?"

I could not say much about that. That I was unusually well educated for my years there could be no doubt about, especially in the classics and French. My father had laid a good foundation to begin with, and the school chosen for me was a first-rate one. The French resident master had taken a liking to me, and had me much with him. Once during the midsummer holidays he had taken me to stay with his people in France: to Abbeville, with its interesting old church and market-place, its quaint costumes and uncomfortable inns. Altogether, I spoke and wrote French almost as well as he did.

"What are they going to make of you, Charley? Is it as old Stillingfar pleases?"

"I think so. I dare say they'll put me to the law."

"Unfortunate martyr! I'd rather command a pirate-boat on the high seas than stew my brains over dry law-books and musty parchments!"

"Tastes differ," struck in Miss Blanche. "And you are not going to sea at all, Tom."

"Tastes do differ," smiled Mrs. Carlen. "I should think it much nicer to harangue judges and law-courts in a silk gown and wig, Tom, than to put on a red coat and go out to be shot at."

"Hark at the mamsie!" cried Tom, laughing. "Charley, give me some more tongue. Where's the Major to-night?"

The Major was dining out. Tom and I were always best pleased when he did dine out. A pompous, boasting sort of man, I did not like him at all. As Tom put it, we would at any time rather have his room than his company.

The days I am writing of are not these days. Boys left school earlier then than they do now. I suppose education was not so comprehensive as it is now made: but it served us. It was quite a usual thing to place a lad out in the world at fourteen or fifteen, whether to a profession or a trade.

Therefore little surprise was caused at home by notice having been given of my removal from school.

At breakfast, next morning, Tom began laying out plans for the day. "I'll take you to this thing, Charley, and I'll take you to that." Major Carlen sat in his usual place at the foot of the table, facing his wife. An imposing-looking man, tall, thin and angular, who must formerly have been handsome. He had a large nose with a curious twist in it; white teeth, which he showed very much; light gray eyes that stared at you, and hair and whiskers of so brilliant a black that a suspicious person might have said they were dyed.

"I thought of taking you boys out myself this afternoon," spoke the Major. "To see that horsemanship which is exhibiting. I hear it's very good. Would you like to go?"

"Oh, and me too!" struck in Blanche. "Take me, papa."

"No," answered the Major, after reflection. "I don't consider it a fit place for little girls. Would you boys like to go?" he asked.

We said we should like it; said it in a sort of surprise, for it was almost the first time he had ever offered to take us anywhere.

"Charles cannot go," hastily interrupted Mrs. Carlen, who had at length opened a letter which had been lying beside her plate. "This is from Mr. Serjeant Stillingfar, Charley. He asks me to send you to his chambers this afternoon. You are to be there at three o'clock."

"Just like old Stillingfar!" cried Tom resentfully. Considering that he did not know much of Serjeant Stillingfar and had very little experience of his ways, the reproach was gratuitous.

Major Carlen laughed at it. "We must put off the horsemanship to another day," said he. "It will come to the same thing. I will take you out somewhere instead, Blanchie."

Taking an omnibus in Oxford Street, when lunch was over, I went down to Holborn, and thence to Lincoln's Inn. The reader may hardly believe that I had never been to my uncle's chambers before, though I had sometimes been to his house. He seemed to have kept me at a distance. His rooms were on the first floor. On the outer door I read "Mr. Serjeant Stillingfar."

"Come in," cried out a voice, in answer to my knock. And I entered a narrow little room.

A pert-looking youth with a quantity of long, light curly hair and an eye-glass, and not much older than myself, sat on a stool at a desk, beside an unoccupied chair. He eyed me from head to foot. I wore an Eton jacket and turn-down collar; he wore a "tail" coat, a stand-up collar, and a stock.

"What do *you* want?" he demanded.

"I want Mr. Serjeant Stillingfar."

"Not in; not to be seen. You can come another day."

"But I am here by appointment."

The young gentleman caught up his eyeglass, fixed it, and turned it on me. "I don't think you are expected," said he coolly.

Now, though he had been gifted with a stock of native impudence, and a very good stock it was at his time of life, I had been gifted with native modesty. I waited in silence, not knowing what to do. Two or three chairs stood about. He no doubt would have tried them all in succession, had it suited him to do so. I did not like to take one of them.

"Will my uncle be long, do you know?" I asked.

"Who *is* your uncle?"

"Mr. Serjeant Stillingfar."

He put up his glass again, which had dropped, and stared at me harder than before. At this juncture an inner door was opened, and a middle-aged man in a black coat and white neckcloth came through it.

"Are you Mr. Strange?" he inquired, quietly and courteously.

"Yes. My uncle, Mr. Serjeant Stillingfar, wrote to tell me to be here at three o'clock."

"I know. Will you step in here? The Serjeant is in Court, but will not be long. As to you, young Mr. Lake, if you persist in exercising your impudent tongue upon all comers, I shall request the Serjeant to put a stop to your sitting here at all. How many times have you been told not to take upon yourself to answer callers, but to refer them to me when Michael is out?"

"About a hundred and fifty, I suppose, old Jones. Haven't counted them, though," retorted Mr. Lake.

"Impertinent young rascal!" ejaculated Mr. Jones, as he took me into the next room, and turned to a little desk that stood in a corner. He was the Serjeant's confidential clerk, and had been with him for years. Arthur Lake, beginning to read for the Bar, was allowed by the Serjeant and his clerk to sit in their chambers of a day, to pick up a little experience.

"Sit down by the fire, Mr. Strange," said the clerk. "It is a warm day, though, for the season. I expected the Serjeant in before this. He will not be long now."

Before I had well taken in the bearings of the room, which was the Serjeant's own, and larger and better than the other, he came in, wearing his silk gown and gray wig. He was a little man, growing elderly now, with a round, smooth, fair face, out of which twinkled kindly blue eyes. Mr. Jones got up from his desk at once to divest him of wig and gown, producing at the same time a miniature flaxen wig, which the Serjeant put upon his head.

"So you have come, Charles!" he said, shaking hands with me as he sat down in a large elbow-chair. Mr. Jones went out with his arm full of papers and shut the door upon us.

"Yes, sir," I answered.

"You will be sixteen next May, I believe," he added. He had the mildest voice and manner imaginable; not at all what might be expected in a serjeant-at-law, who was supposed to take the Court by storm on occasion. "And I understand from your late master that in all your studies you are remarkably well advanced."

"Pretty well, I think, sir," I answered modestly.

"Ay. I am glad to hear you speak of it in a diffident, proper sort of way. Always be modest, lad; true merit ever is so. It tells, too, in the long-run. Well, Charles, I think it time that you were placed out in life."

"Yes, sir."

"Is there any calling that you especially fancy? Any one profession you would prefer to embrace above another?"

"No, sir; I don't know that there is. I have always had an idea that it would be the law. I think I should like that."

"Just so," he answered, the faint pink on his smooth cheeks growing deeper with gratification. "It is what I have always intended you to enter—provided you had no insuperable objection to it. But I shall not make a barrister of you, Charles."

"No!" I exclaimed. "What then?"

"An attorney-at-law."

I was too much taken by surprise to answer at once. "Is that—a gentleman's calling, Uncle Charles?" I at length took courage to ask.

"Ay, that it is, lad," he impressively rejoined. "It's true you've no chance of the Woolsack or of a judgeship, or even of becoming a pleader, as I am. If you had a ready-made fortune, Charles, you might eat your dinners, get called, and risk it. But you have not; and I will not be the means of condemning the best years of your life to anxious poverty."

I only looked at him, without speaking. I fancy he must have seen disappointment in my face.

"Look here, Charles," he resumed, bending forward impressively: "I will tell you a little of my past experience. My people thought they were doing a great thing for me when they put me to the Bar. I thought the same. I was called in due course, and donned my stuff gown and wig in glory—the glory cast by the glamour of hope. How long my mind maintained that glamour; how long it was before it began to give place to doubt; how many years it took to merge doubt into despair, I cannot tell you. I think something like fifteen or twenty."

"Fifteen or twenty years, Uncle Stillingfar!"

"Not less. I was steady, persevering, sufficiently clever. Yet practice did not come to me. It is all a lottery. I had no fortune, lad; no one to help me. I was not clever at writing for the newspapers and magazines, as many of my fellows were. And for more years than I care to recall I had a hard struggle for existence. I was engaged to be married. She was a sweet, patient girl, and we waited until we were both bordering upon middle age. Ay, Charles, I was forty years old before practice began to flow in upon me. The long lane had taken a turning at last. It flew in then with a vengeance—more work than I could possibly undertake."

"And did you marry the young lady, Uncle Charles?" I asked in the pause he came to. I had never heard of his having a wife.

"No, child; she was dead. I think she died of waiting."

I drew a long breath, deeply interested.

"There are scores of young fellows starving upon hope now, as I starved then, Charles. The market is terribly overstocked. For ten barristers striving to rush into note in my days, you may count twenty or thirty in these. I will not have you swell the lists. My brother's grandson shall never, with my consent, waste his best years in fighting with poverty, waiting for luck that may never come to him."

"I suppose it is a lottery, as you say, sir."

"A lottery where blanks far outweigh the prizes," he assented. "A lottery into which you shall not enter. No, Charles; you shall be spared that. As a lawyer, I can make your progress tolerably sure. You may be a rich man in time if you will, and an honourable one. I have sounded my old friend, Henry Brightman, and I think he is willing to take you."

"I am afraid I should not make a good pleader, sir," I acknowledged, falling in with his views. "I can't speak a bit. We had a debating-club at school, and in the middle of a speech I always lost myself."

He nodded, and rose. "You shall not try it, my boy. And that's all for to-day, Charles. All I wanted was to sound your views before making arrangements with Brightman."

"Has he a good practice, sir?"

"He has a very large and honourable practice, Charles. He is a good man and a *gentleman*," concluded the Serjeant emphatically. "All being well, you may become his partner sometime."

"Am I not to go to Oxford, sir?" I asked wistfully.

"If you particularly wish to do so and circumstances permit it, you may perhaps keep a few terms when you are out of your articles," he replied, with hesitation. "We shall see, Charles, when that time comes."

"What a shame!" exclaimed Mrs. Carlen, when I reached home. "Make you a lawyer! That he never shall, Charles. I shall not allow it. I will go down and remonstrate with him."

Major Carlen said it was a shame; said it contemptuously. Tom said it was a double-shame, and threw a host of hard words upon Mr. Serjeant Stillingfar. Blanche began to cry. She had been reading that day about a press-gang, and quite believed my fate would be worse than that of being pressed.

After breakfast, next morning, we hastened to Lincoln's Inn: I and Mrs. Carlen, for she kept her word. I should be a barrister or nothing, she protested. All very fine to say so! She had no power over me whatever. That lay with Mr. Serjeant Stillingfar and the other trustee, and he never interfered. If they chose to article me to a chimneysweep instead of a lawyer, no one could say them nay.

Mr. Jones and young Lake sat side by side at the desk in the first room when we arrived. Mr. Serjeant Stillingfar was in his own room. He received us very kindly, shaking hands with Mrs. Carlen, whom he had seen occasionally. Mrs. Carlen, sitting opposite to him, entered upon her protest, and was meekly listened to by the Serjeant.

"Better be a successful attorney, madam, than a briefless barrister," he observed, when she finished.

"All barristers are not briefless," said Mrs. Carlen.

"A great many of them are," he answered. "Some of them never make their mark at all; they live and die struggling men." And, leaning forward in his chair—as he had leaned towards me yesterday—he repeated a good deal that he had then said of his own history; his long-continued poverty, and his despairing struggles. Mrs. Carlen's heart melted.

"Yes, I know. It is very sad, dear Mr. Serjeant, and I am sure your experience is only that of many others," she sighed. "But, if I understand the matter rightly, the chief trouble of these young barristers is their poverty. Had they means to live, they could wait patiently and comfortably until success came to them."

"Of course," he assented. "It is the want of private means that makes the uphill path so hard."

"Charles has his three hundred a year."

The faint pink in his cheeks, just the hue of a sea-shell, turned to crimson. I was sitting beyond the table, and saw it. He glanced across at me.

"It will take more money to make Charles a lawyer and to ensure him a footing afterwards in a good house than it would to get him called to the Bar," he said with a smile.

"Yes—perhaps so. But that is not quite the argument, Mr. Serjeant," said my stepmother. "Any young man who has three hundred a year may manage to live upon it."

"It is to be hoped so. I know I should have thought three hundred a year a perfect gold-mine."

"Then you see Charles need not starve while waiting for briefs to come in to him. Do you *not* see that, Mr. Serjeant?"

"I see it very clearly," he mildly said. "Had Charles his three hundred a year to fall back upon, he might have gone to the Bar had he liked, and risked the future."

"But he has it," Mrs. Carlen rejoined, surprise in her tone.

"No, madam, he has it not. Nor two hundred a year, nor one hundred."

They silently looked at one another for a full minute. Mrs. Carlen evidently could not understand his meaning. I am sure I did not.

"Charles's money, I am sorry to say, is lost," he continued.

"Lost! Since when?"

"Since the bank-panic that we had nearly two years ago."

Mrs. Carlen collapsed. "Oh, dear!" she breathed. "Did you—pray forgive the question, Mr. Serjeant—did you lose it? Or—or—the other trustee?"

He shook his head. "No, no. We neither lost it, nor are we responsible for the loss. Charles's grandfather, my brother, invested the money, six thousand pounds, in bank debentures to bring in five per cent. He settled the money upon his daughter, Lucy, and upon her children after her, making myself and our old friend, George Wickham, trustees. In the panic of two years ago this bank *went*; its shares and its debentures became all but worthless."

"Is the money all gone? quite gone?" gasped Mrs. Carlen. "Will it never be recovered?"

"The debentures are Charles's still, but they are for the present almost worthless," he replied. "The bank went on again, and if it can recover itself and regain prosperity, Charles in the end may not greatly suffer. He may regain his money, or part of it. But it will not be yet awhile. The unused portion of the income had been sunk, year by year, in further debentures, in accordance with the directions of the will. All went."

"But—someone must have paid for Charles all this time—two whole years!" she reiterated, in vexed surprise.

"Yes! it has been managed," he gently said.

"I think you must have paid for him yourself," spoke Mrs. Carlen with impulse. "I think it is you who are intending to pay the premium to Mr. Brightman, and to provide for his future expenses? You are a good man, Mr. Serjeant Stillingfar!"

His face broke into a smile: the rare sweet smile which so seldom crossed it. "I am only lending it to him. Charley will repay me when he is a rich man. But you see now, Mrs. Carlen, why a certainty will be better for him than an uncertainty."

We saw it all too clearly, and there was no more remonstrance to be made. Mrs. Carlen rose to leave, just as Mr. Jones came bustling into the room.

"Time is up, sir," he said to his master. "The Court will be waiting."

"Ah, so: is it? Good-morning, madam," he added, politely dismissing her. "I shall send for you here again in a day or two, Charles."

"Thank you for what you are doing for me, Uncle Charles," I whispered. "It is very kind of you."

He laid his hand upon my shoulder affectionately, keeping it there for a few seconds. And as we went out, the last glimpse I had was of his kind, gentle face, and Mr. Jones standing ready to assist him on with his wig and gown.

And we went back to Gloucester Place aware that my destiny in life was settled.

CHAPTER IV
IN ESSEX STREET

HENRY BRIGHTMAN'S offices were in Essex Street, Strand, near the Temple. He rented the whole house: a capital house, towards the bottom of the street on the left-hand side as you go down. His father, who had been head and chief of the firm, had lived in it. But old Mr. Brightman was dead, and his son, now sole master, lived over the water on the Surrey side, in a style his father would never have dreamt of. It was a firm of repute and consideration; and few legal firms, if any, in London were better regarded.

It was to this gentleman my uncle, Mr. Serjeant Stillingfar, articled me: and a gentleman Henry Brightman was in every sense of the term. He was a slender man of middle height, with a bright, pleasant face, quick, dark eyes, and brown hair. Very much to my surprise, I found, when arrangements were being made for me, that I was to live in the house. Serjeant Stillingfar had made it a condition that I should do so. He and the late Mr. Brightman had been firm friends, and his friendship was continued to Henry. An old lady, one Miss Methold, a cousin of the Brightmans, resided in the house, and I was to take up my abode with her. She was a kind old thing, though a little stern and reserved, and she made me very comfortable.

There were several clerks; and one articled pupil, who was leaving the house as I entered it. The head of all was a gentleman named Lennard, who seemed to take all management upon himself, under Mr. Brightman. George Lennard was a tall spare man, with a thin, fair, aristocratic face and well-formed features. He looked about thirty-five years old, and an impression prevailed in the office that he was well-born, well-connected, and had come down in the world through loss of fortune. A man of few words, attentive, and always at his post, Lennard was an excellent superintendent, ruling with a strict yet kindly hand.

One day, some weeks after I had entered, as I was at dinner with Miss Methold in her sitting-room, and the weather was warm enough for all doors to be open, we heard horses and carriage-wheels dash up to the house. The room was at the head of the stairs, leading from the offices to the kitchen: a large, pleasant room with a window looking towards the Temple chambers and the winding river.

"What a commotion!" exclaimed Miss Methold.

I went to the door, and saw an open barouche, with a lady and a little girl inside it, attended by a coachman and footman in livery.

"It is quite a grand carriage, Miss Methold."

"Oh," said she, looking over my shoulder: "it is Mrs. Brightman."

"Very proud and high-and-mighty, is she not?" I rejoined, for the clerks had talked about her.

"She was born proud. Her mother was a nobleman's daughter, and she'll be proud to the end," said the old lady. "Henry keeps up great show and state for her. Of course, that is his affair, not mine."

"I hear he has a charming place at Clapham, Miss Methold?"

"So do I," she answered rather bitterly. "I have never seen it."

"Never seen it?" I echoed in surprise.

"Never," she answered. "I have not even been invited there by her. Never once, Charles. Mrs. Brightman despises her husband's profession in her heart; she despises me as belonging to it, I suppose, and as a poor relation. She has never condescended to get out of her carriage to enter the office here, and has never asked to see me, here or there. Henry has invited me down there once or twice when she was away from home, but I have said, No, thank you."

Mr. Lennard came in. The clerks, one excepted, had gone out to dinner. "Do you know whether it will be long before Mr. Brightman comes in, or where he has gone to?" he said to Miss Methold.

"Indeed, I do not," she answered rather shortly. "I only knew he was out by his not appearing now at luncheon."

"Charles, go to the carriage and tell Mrs. Brightman that we don't know how long it may be before Mr. Brightman comes in," said he.

I rather wondered why he could not go himself as I took out the message to Mrs. Brightman.

She had a fair proud face, and her air was cold and haughty as she listened to me.

"Let this be given to him as soon as he comes in," she said, handing me a sealed note. "Regent Street; Carbonell's," she added to the footman.

As the carriage turned and bowled away, I caught the child's pretty face, a smile on her rosy lips and in her laughing brown eyes.

I may as well say here that young Lake had struck up an acquaintanceship with me. The reader may remember that I saw him at the chambers of Mr. Serjeant Stillingfar. I grew to like him greatly. His faults were all on the surface; his heart was in the right place. Boy though he was, he was thrown upon himself in the world. I don't mean as to money, but as to a home; and he steered his course unscathed through its shoals. The few friends he had lived in the country. He had neither father nor mother. His lodgings were in Norfolk Street, very near to us. Miss Methold would sometimes have him in to spend Sunday with me; and now and then, but very rarely, he and I were invited for that day to dine with Mr. Serjeant Stillingfar.

The Serjeant lived in Russell Square, in one of its handsomest houses. But he kept, so to say, no establishment; just two or three servants and a modest little brougham. He must have been making a great deal of money at that time, and I suppose he put it by.

"Ah! you don't know, Charley," Lake said to me one evening when I was in Norfolk Street, and we began talking of him. "It is said his money went in that same precious bank which devoured yours; and it is thought that he lives in this quiet manner, eschewing pomps and vanities, to be able to help friends who were quite ruined by it. Old Jones knows a little, and I've heard him drop a word or two."

"I am sure my uncle is singularly good and kind. Those simple-minded men generally are."

Lake nodded. "Few men, *I* should say, come up to Serjeant Stillingfar."

A trouble had come to me in the early spring. I thought it a great one, and grieved over it. Major Carlen gave up his house in Gloucester Place, letting it furnished for a long term, and went abroad with his wife. *He* might have gone to the end of the world for ever and a day, but she was like my second mother, and indeed *was* so, and I felt lost without her. They took up their abode at Brussels. It would be good for Blanche's education, Mrs. Carlen wrote to me. Other people said that the Major had considerably out-run the constable, and went there to economise. Tom Heriot was down at Portsmouth with his regiment.

I think that is all I need say of this part of my life. I liked my profession very much indeed, and got on well in it and with Mr. Brightman and the clerks, and with good old Miss Methold. And so the years passed on.

The first change came when I was close upon twenty years of age: came in the death of Miss Methold. After that, I left Essex Street as a residence, for there was no longer anyone to rule it, and went into Lake's lodgings in Norfolk Street, sharing his sitting-room and securing a bedroom. And still a little more time rolled on.

It was Easter-tide. On Easter Eve, it happened that I had remained in the office after the other clerks had left, to finish some work in hand. In these days Saturday afternoon has become a general holiday; in those days we had to work all the harder. On Saturdays a holiday was unknown.

Writing steadily, I finished my task, and was locking up my desk, which stood near the far window in the front room on the ground floor, when Mr. Brightman, who had also remained late, came downstairs from his private room, and looked in.

"Not gone yet, Charley!"

"I am going now, sir. I have only just finished my work."

"Some of the clerks are coming on Monday, I believe," continued Mr. Brightman. "Are you one of them?"

"Yes, sir. Mr. Lennard told me I might take holiday, but I did not care about it. As I have no friends to spend it with, it would not be much of a holiday to me. Arthur Lake is out of town."

"And Mr. Serjeant Stillingfar on circuit," added Mr. Brightman.

He paused and looked at me, as he stood near the door. I was gathering the pens together.

"Have you no friends to dine with, to-morrow—Easter Day?"

"No, sir. At least, I have not been asked anywhere. I think I shall go for a blow up the river."

"A blow up the river!" he repeated doubtfully. "Don't you go to church?"

"Always. I go to the Temple. I meant in the afternoon, sir."

"Well, if you have no friends to dine with, you may come and dine with me," said Mr. Brightman, after a moment's consideration. "Come down when service is over. You will find an omnibus at Charing Cross."

The invitation pleased me. Some of the clerks would have given their ears for it. Of course I mean the gentlemen clerks; not one of whom had ever been so favoured. I had sometimes wondered that he never asked me, considering his intimacy with my uncle. But, I suppose, to have invited me to his house and left out Miss Methold would have been rather too pointed a slight upon her.

It was a fine day. The Temple service was beautiful, as usual; the anthem, "I know that my Redeemer liveth." Afterwards I went forth to keep my engagement, and in due time reached the entrance-gates of Mr. Brightman's residence.

It was a large, handsome villa, enclosed in fine pleasure-grounds, near Clapham. They lived in a good deal of style, kept seven or eight servants and two carriages: a large barouche, and a brougham in which he sometimes came to town. A well-appointed house, full of comfort and luxury. Mr. Brightman was on the lawn when I reached it.

"Well, Charles! I began to think you were late."

"I walked down, sir. The first two omnibuses were full, and I would not wait for a third."

"Rather a long walk," he remarked with a smile. "But it is what I should have done at your age. Dinner will be ready soon. We dine at three o'clock on Sundays. It allows ourselves and the servants to attend evening as well as morning service."

He had walked towards the house as he spoke, and we went in. The drawing-room and dining-room opened on either side a large hall. In the former room sat Mrs. Brightman. I had seen her occasionally at the office door in her carriage, but had never spoken to her except that first time. She was considerably younger than Mr. Brightman, who must have been then getting towards fifty. A proud woman she looked as she sat there; her hair light and silky, her blue eyes disdainful, her dress a rich purple silk, with fine white lace about it.

"Here is Charles Strange at last," Mr. Brightman said to her, and she replied by a slight bend of the head. She did not offer to shake hands with me.

"I have heard of you as living in Essex Street," she condescended to observe, as I sat down. "Your relatives do not, I presume, live in London?"

"I have not any near relatives," was my answer. "My great-uncle lives in London, but he is away just now."

"You were speaking of that great civil cause, Emma, lately tried in the country; and of the ability of the defendants' counsel, Serjeant Stillingfar," put in Mr. Brightman. "It is Serjeant Stillingfar, if you remember, who is Charles's uncle."

"Oh, indeed," she said; and I thought her manner became rather more gracious. And ah, what a gracious, charming lady she could be when she pleased!—when she was amongst people whom she considered of her own rank and degree.

"Where is Annabel?" asked Mr. Brightman.

"She has gone dancing off somewhere," was Mrs. Brightman's reply. "I never saw such a child. She is never five minutes together in one place."

Presently she danced in. A graceful, pretty child, apparently about twelve, in a light-blue silk frock. She wore her soft brown hair in curls round her head, and they flew about as she flew, and a bright colour rose to her cheeks with every word she spoke, and her eyes were like her father's—dark, tender, expressive. Not any resemblance could I trace to her mother, unless it lay in the same delicately-formed features.

We had a plain dinner; a quarter of lamb, pastry and creams. Mr. Brightman did not exactly apologize for it, but explained that on Sundays they had as little cooking as possible. But it was handsomely served, and there were several sorts of wine. Three servants waited at table, two in livery and the butler in plain clothes.

Some little time after it was over, Mr. Brightman left the room, and Mrs. Brightman, without the least ceremony, leaned back in an easy-chair and closed her eyes. I said something to the child. She did not answer, but came to me on tiptoe.

"If we talk, mamma will be angry," she whispered. "She never lets me make a noise while she goes to sleep. Would you like to come out on the lawn? We may talk there."

I nodded, and Annabel silently opened and passed out at one of the French windows, holding it back for me. I as silently closed it.

"Take care that it is quite shut," she said, "or the draught may get to mamma. Papa has gone to his room to smoke his cigar," she continued; "and we shall have coffee when mamma awakes. We do not take tea until after church. Shall you go to church with us?"

"I dare say I shall. Do you go?"

"Of course I do. My governess tells me never to miss attending church twice on Sundays, unless there is very good cause for doing so, and then things will go well with me in the week. But if I wished to stay at home, papa would not let me. Once, do you know, I made an excuse to stay away from morning service: I said my head ached badly, though it did not. It was to read a book that had been lent me, 'The Old English Baron.' I feared my governess would not let me read it, if she saw it, because it was about ghosts, so that I had only the Sunday to read it in. Well, do you know, that next week nothing went right with me; my lessons were turned back, my drawing was spoilt, and my French mistress tore my translation in two. Oh, dear! it was nothing but scolding and crossness. So at last, on the Saturday, I burst into tears and told Miss Shelley about staying away from church and the false excuse I had made. But she was very kind, and would not punish me, for she said I had already had a whole week of punishment."

Of all the little chatterboxes! "Is Miss Shelley your governess now?" I asked her.

"Yes. But her mother is an invalid, so mamma allows her to go home every Saturday night and come back on Monday morning. Mamma says it is pleasant to have Sunday to ourselves. But I like Miss Shelley very much, and should be dull without her if papa were not at home. I do love Sundays, because papa's here. Did you ever read 'The Old English Baron'?"

"No."

"Shall I lend it you to take home?" continued Annabel, her cheeks glowing, her eyes sparkling with good-nature. "I have it for my own now. It is a very nice book. Have your sisters read it? Perhaps you have no sisters?"

"I have no real sisters, and my father and mother are dead. I have—"

"Oh dear, how sad!" interrupted Annabel, clasping her hands. "Not to have a father and mother! Was it"—after a pause—"you who lived with Miss Methold?"

"Yes. Did you know her?"

"I knew her; and I liked her—oh, very much. Papa used to take me to see her sometimes. With whom do you live now?"

"I live in lodgings."

She stood looking at me with her earnest eyes—thoughtful eyes just then.

"Then who sews the buttons on your shirts?"

I burst into laughter: the reader may have done the same. "My landlady professes to sew them on, Annabel, but the shirts often go without buttons. Sometimes I sew one on myself."

"If you had one off now, and it was not Sunday, I would sew it on for you," said Annabel. "Why do you laugh?"

"At your concern about my domestic affairs, my dear little girl."

"But there's a gentleman who lives in lodgings and comes here sometimes to dine with papa—he is older than you—and he says it is the worst trouble of life to have no one to sew his buttons on. Who takes care of you if you are ill?" she added, after another pause.

"As there is no one to take care of me, I cannot afford to be ill, Annabel. I am generally quite well."

"I am glad of that. Was your father a lawyer, like papa?"

"No. He was a clergyman."

"Oh, don't turn," she cried; "I want to show you my birds. We have an aviary, and they are beautiful. Papa lets me call them mine; and some of them are mine in reality, for they were bought for me. Mamma does not care for birds."

Presently I asked Annabel her age.

"Fourteen."

"Fourteen!" I exclaimed in surprise.

"I was fourteen in January. Mamma says I ought not to tell people my age, for they will only think me more childish; but papa says I may tell everyone."

She was in truth a child for her years; especially as age is now considered. She ran about, showing me everything, her frock, her curls, her eyes dancing: from the aviary to the fowls, from the fowls to the flowers: all innocent objects of her daily pleasures, innocent and guileless as she herself.

A smart-looking maid, with red ringlets flowing about her red cheeks, and wide cap-strings flowing behind them, came up.

"Why, here you are!" she exclaimed. "I've been looking all about for you, Miss Annabel. Your mamma says you are to come in."

"We are coming, Hatch; we were turning at that moment," answered the child. "Is coffee ready?"

"Yes, Miss Annabel, and waiting."

In the evening we went to church, the servants following at some distance. Afterwards we had tea, and then I rose to depart. Mr. Brightman walked with me across the lawn, and we had almost reached the iron gates when there came a sound of swift steps behind us.

"Papa! papa! Is he gone? Is Mr. Strange gone?"

"What is the matter now?" asked Mr. Brightman.

"I promised to lend Mr. Strange this: it is 'The Old English Baron.' He has never read it."

"There, run back," said Mr. Brightman, as I turned and took the book from her. "You will catch cold, Annabel."

"What a charming child she is, sir!" I could not help exclaiming.

"She is that," he replied. "A true child of nature, knowing no harm and thinking none. Mrs. Brightman complains that her ideas and manners are unformed; no style about her, she says, no reserve. In my opinion that ought to constitute a child's chief charm. All Annabel's parts are good. Of sense, intellect, talent, she possesses her full share; and I am thankful that they are not prematurely developed. I am thankful," he repeated with emphasis, "that she is not a forward child. In my young days, girls were girls, but now there is not such a thing to be found. They are all women. I do not admire the forcing system myself; forced vegetables, forced fruit, forced children: they are good for little. A genuine child, such as Annabel, is a treasure rarely met with."

I thought so too.

CHAPTER V
WATTS'S WIFE

LEAVING the omnibus at Charing Cross, I was hastening along the Strand on my way home, when I ran against a gentleman, who was swaggering along in a handsome, capacious cloak as if all the street belonged to him.

"I beg your pardon," I said, in apology. "I—" And there I broke off to stare, for I thought I recognised him in the gaslight.

"Why! It is Major Carlen!"

"Just so. And it is Charles. How are you, Charles?"

"Have you lately come from Brussels?" I asked, as we shook hands. "And how did you leave mamma and Blanche?"

"They are in Gloucester Place," he answered. "We all came over last Wednesday."

"I wonder they did not let me know it."

"Plenty of time, young man. They will not be going away in a hurry. We are settling down here again. You can come up when you like."

"That will be to-morrow then. Good-night, sir."

But it was not until Monday evening that I could get away. Mr. Lennard went out in the afternoon on some private matter of his own, and desired me to remain in to see a client, who had sent us word he should call, although it was Easter Monday. Mr. Brightman did not come to town that day.

Six o'clock was striking when I reached Gloucester Place. Blanche ran to meet me in the passage, and we had a spell of kissing. I think she was then about fourteen; perhaps fifteen. A fair, upright, beautiful girl, with the haughty blue eyes of her childhood, and a shower of golden curls.

"Oh, Charley, I am so glad! I thought you were never, never coming to us."

"I did not know you were here until last night. You should have sent me word."

"I told mamma so; but she was not well. She is not well yet. The journey tired her, you see, and the sea was rough. Come upstairs and see her, Charley. Papa has just gone out."

Mrs. Carlen sat over the fire in the drawing-room in an easy-chair, a shawl upon her shoulders. It was a dull evening, twilight not far off, and she sat with her back to the light. It struck me she looked thin and ill. I had been over once or twice to stay with them in Brussels; the last time, eighteen months ago.

"Are you well, mamma?" I asked as she kissed me—for I had not left off calling her by the fond old childhood's name. "You don't look so."

"The journey tired me, Charley," she answered—just as Blanche had said to me. "I have a little cold, too. Sit down, my boy."

"Have you come back here for good?" I asked.

"Well, yes, I suppose so," she replied with hesitation. "For the present, at all events."

Tea was brought in. Blanche made it; her mother kept to her chair and her shawl. The more I looked at her, the greater grew the conviction that something beyond common ailed her. Major Carlen was dining out, and they had dined in the middle of the day.

Alas! I soon knew what was wrong. After tea, contriving to get rid of Blanche for a few minutes on some plausible excuse, she told me all. An inward complaint was manifesting itself, and it was hard to say how it might terminate. The Belgian doctors had not been very reassuring upon the point. On the morrow she was going to consult James Paget.

"Does Blanche know?" I asked.

"Not yet. I must see Mr. Paget before saying anything to her. If my own fears are confirmed, I shall tell her. In that case I shall lose no time in placing her at school."

"At school!"

"Why, yes, Charley. What else can be done? This will be no home for her when I am out of it. Not at an ordinary school, though. I shall send her to our old home, White Littleham Rectory. Mr. and Mrs. Ravensworth are there still. She takes two or three pupils to bring up with her own daughter, and will be glad of Blanche. There—we will put that subject away for the present, Charley. I want to ask you about something else, and Blanche will soon be back again. Do you see much of Tom Heriot?"

"I see him very rarely indeed. He is not quartered in London, you know."

"Charles, I am afraid—I am very much afraid that Tom is wild," she went on, after a pause. "He came into his money last year: six thousand pounds. We hear that he has been launching out into all sorts of extravagance ever since. That must mean that he is drawing on his capital."

I had heard a little about Tom's doings myself. At least, Lake had done so, which came to the same thing. But I did not say this.

"It distresses me much, Charles. You know how careless and improvident Tom is, and yet how generous-hearted. He will bring himself to ruin if he does not mind, and what would become of him then? Major Carlen says—Hush! here comes Blanche."

I cannot linger over this part of my story. Mrs. Carlen died; and Blanche was sent to White Littleham.

And, indeed, of the next few passing years there is not much to record. I obtained my certificate, as a matter of course. Then I managed, by Mr. Brightman's kindness in sparing me, and by my uncle's liberality, to keep a few terms at Oxford. I was twenty-three when I kept the last term, and then I was sent for some months to Paris, to make myself acquainted with law as administered in the French courts. That over, arrangements were made for my becoming Mr. Brightman's partner. If he had had sons, one of them would probably have filled the position. Having none, he admitted me on easy terms, for I had my brains about me, as the saying runs, and was excessively useful to the firm. A certain sum was paid down by Mr. Serjeant Stillingfar, and the firm became Brightman and Strange. I was to receive at first only a small portion of the profits. And let me say here, that all my expenses of every description, during these past years, had been provided for by that good man, Charles Stillingfar, and provided liberally. So there I was in an excellent position, settled for life when only twenty-four years of age.

After coming home from Paris to enter upon these new arrangements, I found Mr. Brightman had installed a certain James Watts in Essex Street as care-taker and messenger, our former man, Dickory, having become old and feeble. A good change. Dickory, in growing old, had grown fretful and obstinate, and liked his own way and will better than that of his masters. Watts was well-mannered and well-spoken; respectable and trustworthy. His wife's duties were to keep the rooms clean, in which she was at liberty to have in a woman to help once or twice a week if she so minded, and up to the present time to prepare Mr. Brightman's daily luncheon. They lived in the rooms on the bottom floor, one of which was their bedroom.

"I like them both," I said to Mr. Brightman, when I had been back a day or two. "Things will be comfortable now."

"Yes, Charles; I hope you will find them so," he answered.

For it ought to be mentioned that, in becoming Mr. Brightman's partner, it had been settled that I should return as an inmate to the house. He said he should prefer it. And, indeed, I thought I should also. So that I had taken up my abode there at once.

The two rooms on the ground floor were occupied by the clerks. Mr. Lennard had his desk in the back one. Miss Methold's parlour, a few steps lower, was now not much used, except that a client was sometimes taken into it. The large front room on the first floor was Mr. Brightman's private room; the back one was mine; but he had also a desk in it. These two rooms opened to one another. The floor above this was wholly given over to me; sitting-room, bedroom, and dressing-room. The top floor was only used for boxes, and on those rare occasions when someone wanted to sleep at the office. Watts and his wife were to attend to me; she to see to the meals, he to wait upon me.

"I should let her get in everything without troubling, and bring up the bills weekly, were I you, Charles," remarked Mr. Brightman, one evening when he had stayed later than usual, and was in my room, and we fell to talking of the man and his wife. "Much better than for her to be coming to you everlastingly, saying you want this and you want that. She is honest, I feel sure, and I had the best of characters with both of them."

"She has an honest face," I answered. "But it looks sad. And what a silent woman she is. Speaking of her face though, sir, it puts me in mind of someone's, and I cannot think whose."

"You may have seen her somewhere or other," remarked Mr. Brightman.

"Yes, but I can't remember where. I'll ask her."

Mrs. Watts was then coming into the room with some water, which Mr. Brightman had rung for. She looked about forty-five years old; a thin, bony woman of middle height, with a pale, gray, wrinkled face, and gray hairs banded under a huge cap, tied under her chin.

"There's something about your face that seems familiar to me, Mrs. Watts," I said, as she put down the glass and the bottle of water. "Have I ever seen you before?"

She was pouring out the water, and did not look at me. "I can't say, sir," she answered in a low tone.

"Do you remember *me*? That's the better question."

She shook her head. "Watts and I lived in Ely Place for some years before we came here, sir," she then said. "It's not impossible you may have seen me in the street when I was doing the steps; but I never saw you pass by that I know of."

"And before that, where did you live?"

"Before that, sir? At Dover."

"Ah! well," I said, for this did not help me out with my puzzle; "I suppose it is fancy."

Mr. Brightman caught up the last word as Mrs. Watts withdrew. "Fancy, Charles; that's what it must be. And fancy sometimes plays wonderful tricks with us."

"Yes, sir; I expect it is fancy. For all that, I feel perplexed. The woman's voice and manner seem to strike a chord in my memory as much as her face does."

"Captain Heriot, sir."

Sitting one evening in my room at dusk in the summer weather, the window open to the opposite wall and to the side view of the Thames, waiting for Lake to come in, Watts had thus interrupted me to show in Tom Heriot. I started up and grasped his hands. He was a handsome young fellow, with the open manners that had charmed the world in the days gone by, and charmed it still.

"Charley, boy! It is good to see you."

"Ay, and to see *you*, Tom. Are you staying in London?"

"Why, we have been here for days! What a fellow you are, not to know that we are now quartered here. Don't you read the newspapers? It used to be said, you remember, that young Charley lived in a wood."

I laughed. "And how are things with you, Tom?"

"Rather down; have been for a long time; getting badder and badder."

My heart gave a thump. In spite of his laughing air and bright smile, I feared it might be too true.

"I am going to the deuce, headlong, Charley."

"Don't, Tom!"

"Don't what? Not go or not talk of it? It is as sure as death, lad."

"Have you made holes in your money?"

"Fairly so. I think I may say so, considering that the whole of it is spent."

"Oh, Tom!"

"Every individual stiver. But upon my honour as a soldier, Charley, other people have had more of it than I. A lot of it went at once, when I came into it, paying off back debts."

"What shall you do? You will never make your pay suffice."

"Sell out, I expect."

"And then?"

Tom shrugged his shoulders in answer. They were very slender shoulders. His frame was slight altogether, suggesting that he might not be strong. He was about as tall as I—rather above middle height.

"Take a clerkship with you, at twenty shillings a week, if you'd give it me. Or go out to the Australian diggings to pick up gold. How grave you look, Charles!"

"It is a grave subject. But I hope you are saying this in joke, Tom."

"Half in joke, half in earnest. I will not sell out if I can help it; be sure of that, old man; but I think it will have to come to it. Can you give me something to drink, Charley? I am thirsty."

"Will you take some tea? I am just going to have mine. Or anything else instead?"

"I was thinking of brandy and soda. But I don't mind if I do try tea, for once. Ay, I will. Have it up, Charley."

I rang the bell, and Mrs. Watts brought it up.

"Anything else, sir?" she stayed to ask.

"Not at present. Watts has gone out with that letter, I suppose?— Why, you have forgotten the milk!"

She gave a sharp word at her own stupidity, and left the room. Tom's eyes had been fixed upon her, following her to the last. He began slowly pushing back his bright brown hair, as he would do in his boyhood when anything puzzled him.

"Oh, I remember," he suddenly exclaimed. "So you have *her* here, Charley!"

"Who here?"

"Leah."

"*Leah!* What do you mean?"

"That servant of yours."

"That is our messenger's wife: Mrs. Watts."

"Mrs. Watts she may be now, for aught I know; but she was Leah Williams when we were youngsters, Charley."

"Impossible, Tom. This old woman cannot be Leah."

"I tell you, lad, it is Leah," he persisted. "No mistake about it. At the first moment I did not recollect her. I have a good eye for faces, but she is wonderfully altered. Do you mean to say she has not made herself known to you?"

I shook my head. But even as Tom spoke, little items of remembrance that had worried my brain began to clear themselves bit by bit. Mrs. Watts came in with the milk.

She had put it down on the tray when Tom walked up to her, holding out his hand, his countenance all smiles, his hazel eyes dancing.

"How are you, Leah, after all these years? Shake hands for auld lang syne. Do you sing the song still?"

Leah gave one startled glance and then threw her white apron up to her face with a sob.

"Come, come," said Tom kindly. "I didn't want to startle you, Leah."

"I didn't think you would know me, sir," she said, lifting her woebegone face. "Mr. Charles here did not."

"Not know you! I should know you sooner than my best sweetheart," cried Tom gaily.

"Leah," I interposed, gravely turning to her, "how is it that you did not let me know who you were? Why have you kept it from me?"

She stood with her back against Mr. Brightman's desk, hot tears raining down her worn cheeks.

"I *couldn't* tell you, Master Charles. I'm sorry you know now. It's like a stab to me."

"But why could you not tell me?"

"Pride, I suppose," she shortly said. "I was upper servant at the Rectory; your mamma's own maid, Master Charles: and I couldn't bear you should know that I had come down to this. A servant of all work—scrubbing floors and washing dishes."

"Oh, that's nothing," struck in Tom cheerfully. "Most of us have our ups and downs, Leah. As far as I can foresee, I may be scouring out pots and pans at the gold-diggings next year. I have just been saying so to Mr. Charley. Your second marriage venture was an unlucky one, I expect?"

Leah was crying silently. "No, it is not that," she answered presently in a low tone. "Watts is a steady and respectable man; very much so; above me, if anything. It—it—I have had cares and crosses of my own, Mr. Tom; I have them always; and they keep me down."

"Well, tell me what they are," said Tom. "I may be able to help you. I will if I can."

Leah sighed and moved to the door. "You are just as kind-hearted as ever, Mr. Tom; I see that; and I thank you. Nobody can help me, sir. And my trouble is secret to myself: one I cannot speak of to anyone in the world."

Just as kind-hearted as ever! Yes, Tom Heriot was that, and always would be. Embarrassed as he no doubt was for money, he slipped a gold piece into Leah's hand as she left the room, whispering that it was for old friendship's sake.

And so that was Leah! Back again waiting upon me, as she had waited when I was a child. It was passing strange.

I spoke to her that night, and asked her to confide her trouble to me. The bare suggestion seemed to terrify her.

"It was a dreadful trouble," she admitted in answer; "a nightly and daily torment; one that at times went well-nigh to frighten her senses away. But she must keep it secret, though she died for it."

And as Leah whispered this to me under her breath, she cast dread glances around the walls on all sides, as if she feared that eaves-droppers might be there.

What on earth could the secret be?

And now, for a time, I retire into the background, and cease personally to tell the story.

CHAPTER VI
BLANCHE HERIOT

ON one of those promising days that we now and then see in February, which seem all the more warm and lovely in contrast with the passing winter, the parsonage of White Littleham put on its gayest appearance within—perhaps in response to the fair face of nature without. A group of four girls had collected in the drawing-room. One was taking the brown holland covers from the chairs, sofa, and footstools; another was bringing out certain ornaments, elegant trifles, displayed only on state occasions; the other two were filling glasses with evergreens and hot-house flowers. It was the same room in which you once saw poor Mrs. Strange lying on her road to death. The parsonage received three young ladies to share in the advantages of foreign governesses, provided for the education of its only daughter, Cecilia.

Whilst the girls were thus occupied, a middle-aged lady entered, the mistress of the house, and wife of the Reverend John Ravensworth.

"Oh, Mrs. Ravensworth, why did you come in? We did not want you to see it until it was all finished."

Mrs. Ravensworth smiled. "My dears, it will only look as it has looked many a time before; as it did at Christmas—"

"Mamma, you must excuse my interrupting you," cried the young girl who was arranging the ornaments; "but it will look very different from then. At Christmas we had wretched weather, and see it to-day. And at Christmas we had not the visitors we shall have now."

"We had one of the two visitors, at any rate, Cecilia."

"Oh, yes, we had Arnold. But Arnold is nobody; we are used to him."

"And Major Carlen is somebody," interposed the only beautiful girl present, looking round from the flowers with a laugh. "Thank you, in papa's name, Cecilia."

Very beautiful was she: exceedingly fair, with somewhat haughty blue eyes, delicate features, and fine golden hair. Blanche Heriot (as often as not called Blanche Carlen at the Rectory) stood conspicuous amidst the rest of the girls. They were pleasing-looking and lady-like, but that was all. Rather above middle-height, slender, graceful, she stood as a queen beside her companions. Under different auspices, Blanche Heriot might have become vain and worldly; but, enshrined as she had been for the last few years within the precincts of a humble parsonage, and trained in its doctrines of practical Christianity, Blanche had become thoroughly imbued with the influences around her. Now, in her twentieth year, she was simple and guileless as a child.

It was so long since she had seen her father—as she was pleased to call Major Carlen—that she had partly forgotten what he was like. He was expected now on a two days' visit, and for him the house was being made to look its best. The other visitor, coming by accident at the same time, was Arnold Ravensworth, the Rector's nephew.

Major Carlen's promised visit was an event to the quiet Rector and his wife. All they knew of him was that he was step-father to Blanche, and a man who moved in the gay circles of the world. The interest of Blanche Heriot's money had paid for her education and dress. The Major would have liked the fingering of it amazingly; but to covet is one thing, to obtain is another. Blanche's money was safe in the hands of trustees; but before Mrs. Carlen died she had appointed her husband Blanche's personal guardian, with power to control her residence when she should have attained her eighteenth year. That had been passed some time now, and Major Carlen had just awakened to his responsibilities.

The first to arrive was Arnold Ravensworth, a distinguished-looking man, with a countenance cold, it must be confessed, but full of intellect. And the next to arrive was not the Major. The day passed on to night. The trains came into the neighbouring station, but they did not bring Major Carlen. Blanche cried herself to sleep. She remembered how kind her papa used to be to her—indulging her and taking her about to see sights—and she had cherished a great affection for him. In fact, the Major had always indulged little Blanche.

Neither had he come the next morning. After breakfast, Blanche went to the end of the garden and stood looking out across the field. The shady dingle, where as a little child she had sat to pick violets and primroses, was there; but she was gazing at something else—the path that would bring her father. Arnold Ravensworth came strolling up behind her.

"You know the old saying, Blanche: a watched-for visitor never comes."

"Oh dear, why do you depress me, Arnold? To watch is something. I shall cross the field and look up the road."

They started off in the sunshine. Blanche had a pretty straw hat on. She took the arm Mr. Ravensworth held out to her. Very soon, a stranger turned into the field and came swinging towards them.

"Blanche, is this the Major?"

It was a tall, large-limbed, angular man in an old blue cloak lined with scarlet. He had iron-gray hair and whiskers, gray, hard eyes, a large twisted nose, and very white teeth. Blanche laughed merrily.

"That papa! What an idea you must have of him, Arnold! Papa was a handsome man with black hair, and had lost two of his front teeth. They were knocked out, fighting with the Caffres."

The stranger came on, staring intently at the good-looking young man and the beautiful girl on his arm. Mr. Ravensworth spoke in a low tone.

"Are you quite sure, Blanche? Black hair turns gray, remember; and he has a little travelling portmanteau under that cloak."

Even as he spoke, something in the stranger's face struck upon Blanche Heriot's memory. She disengaged herself and approached him, too agitated to weigh her words.

"Oh—I beg your pardon—are you not papa?"

Major Carlen looked at her closely. "Are you Blanche?"

"Yes, I am Blanche. Oh, papa!"

The Major tucked his step-daughter under his own arm; and Mr. Ravensworth went on to give notice of the arrival.

"Papa, I never saw anyone so much altered!"

"Nor I," interposed the Major. "I was wondering what deuced handsome girl was strolling towards me. You are beautiful, Blanche; more so than your mother was, and she was handsome."

Blanche, confused though she felt at the compliment, could not return it.

"Who is that young fellow?" resumed the Major.

"Arnold Ravensworth; Mr. Ravensworth's nephew. He lives in London, and came down yesterday for a short visit."

"Oh. Does he come often?"

"Pretty often. We wish it was oftener. We like him to be here."

"He seems presuming."

"Dear papa! Presuming! He is not at all so. And he is very talented and clever. He took honours at Oxford, and—"

"I see," interrupted Major Carlen, displaying his large and regular teeth—a habit of his when not pleased. He had rapidly taken up an idea, and it angered him. "Is this the parson, Blanche? He looks very sanctimonious."

"Oh, papa!" she returned, feeling ready to cry at his contemptuous tone. "He is the best man that ever lived. Everyone loves and respects him."

"Hope it's merited, my dear," concluded the Major, as he met the hand of the Reverend John Ravensworth.

Ere middle-day, the Major had scattered a small bombshell through the parsonage by announcing that he had come to take his daughter away. Blanche felt it bitterly. It was her home, and a happy one. To exchange it for the Major's did not look now an inviting prospect. Though she would not acknowledge it to her own heart, she was beginning to regard him with more awe than love. That the resolution must have been suddenly formed she knew, for he had not come down with any intention of removing her.

"Papa, my things can never be ready," was her last forlorn argument, when others had failed.

"Things?" said the Major. "Trunks, and clothes, and rattle-traps? They can be sent after you, Blanche."

"I have a bird," cried Blanche, her eyes filling. "There it is, in the cage."

"Leave it as a souvenir to the Rectory. Blanche, don't be a child. I have pictured you as one hitherto, but now that I see you I find my mistake. You must be thinking of other things, my dear."

And thus Blanche Heriot was hurried away. All the parsonage escorted her to the station, the girls in tears, and she almost heart-broken.

Of late years Major Carlen had been almost always in debt and difficulty. His property was mortgaged. His only certainty was his half-pay; but he was lucky at cards, and often luckier at betting. He retained his club and his visiting connection, and dined out three parts of his time. Just now he was up in the world, having scored a prize on some winter racecourse, and he was back in his house in Gloucester Place. It had been let furnished for three years, portions of which time the Major had spent abroad.

"It will be very dull for me, papa," sighed Blanche, as they were whirling along in an express train. "I dare say you are out all day long, as you used to be."

"Not dull at all," said the Major. "You must make Mrs. Guy take you out and about."

"Mrs. Guy!" exclaimed Blanche, her blue eyes opening widely. "Is she in London?"

"Yes, and a fine old guy she is; more ridiculously nervous than ever," replied the Major. "She arrived unexpectedly from Jersey one evening last week, and quartered herself upon Gloucester Place; for an indefinite period, no doubt. She did this once before, if you remember, in your poor mamma's time."

"She will be something in the way of company for me," said Blanche with another sigh.

"Aye! She is a stupid goose, but you'll be safer under her wing and mine than you would have been ruralising in the fields and the parsonage garden with that Arnold Ravensworth. I have eyes, Miss Blanche."

So had Blanche, especially just then; and they were wide open and fixed upon the Major.

"Doing what, papa?" cried she.

"I saw his drift: 'Blanche' this, and 'Blanche' the other, and his arm put out for you at every turn! No, no; I do not leave you there to be converted into Mrs. Arnold Ravensworth."

Blanche clasped her hands and broke into merry laughter. "Oh, papa, what an idea!—how could you imagine it? Why, he is going to marry Mary Stopford."

Major Carlen looked blank. Had he made all this inconvenient haste for nothing?

"Who the deuce is Mary Stopford?"

"She lives in Devonshire. A pale, gentle girl with nice eyes: I have seen her picture. Arnold wears it attached to a little chain inside his waistcoat. They are to be married in the autumn when the House is up. The very notion of my marrying Arnold Ravensworth!" broke off Blanche with another laugh. A laugh that was quite sufficient to prove the fact that she was heart-whole.

"The House!" repeated the Major. "Who is he, then?"

"He is very well off as to fortune, and is—something. It has to do with the House, not as a Member, though he will be that soon, I believe. I think he is secretary to one of the Ministers. His father was the elder brother, and the

Reverend John Ravensworth the younger. There is a very great difference in their positions. Arnold is well-off, and said to be a rising man."

Every word increased Major Carlen's vexation. Even had his fear been correct, it seemed that the young man would not have been an undesirable match for Blanche, and he had saddled himself with her at a most inconvenient moment!

"Well, well," thought he; "she will soon make her mark, unless I am mistaken, and there's as good fish in the sea as ever came out of it."

Mrs. Guy, widow of the late Admiral Guy, vegetating for years past upon her slight income in Jersey, was Major Carlen's younger sister, and a smaller edition of himself. She had the same generally fair-featured face, with the twisted nose and the gray eyes; but while his eyes were hard and fierce, hers were soft and kindly. She was a well-meaning, but indescribably silly woman; and her nervous fears and fancies had so grown upon her that they were becoming a disease. Lying before the fire on a sofa in her bedroom, she received Blanche with a flood of tears, supplemented by several moans. The tears were caused by the pleased surprise; the moans at her having come home on a Friday, for that must surely betoken ill-luck. Blanche was irreverent enough to laugh.

Major Carlen still counted a few acquaintances of consideration in the social world, and Miss Heriot was introduced to them. Mrs. Guy was persuaded to temporarily forget her ailments, and to act as chaperon. The Major gave his sister a new dress and bonnet, and a cap or two; and as she had not yet quite done with vanity (has a woman *ever* done with it?), she fell before the bribe.

He had been right in his opinion that Blanche's beauty would not fail to make its mark. So charming a girl, so lovely of face and graceful of form, so innocent of guile, had not been seen of late. Before the spring had greatly advanced, a Captain Cross made proposals for her to the Major. He was of excellent family, and offered fair settlements. The Major accepted him, not deeming it at all necessary to consult his daughter.

Blanche rebelled. "I don't care for him, papa," she objected.

The Major gave his nose a twist. He did not intend to have any trouble with Blanche, and would not allow her to begin it.

"Not care!" he exclaimed in surprise. "What does that matter? Captain Cross is a fine man, stands six feet one, and you'll care for him in time."

"But, before I consent to marry him, I ought to know whether I shall like him or not."

"Blanche, you are a dunce! You have been smothered up in that parsonage till you know nothing. Do you suppose that in our class of society it is usual to fall in love, as the ploughboys and milkmaids do? People marry first, and grow accustomed to each other afterwards. Whatever you do, my dear, don't betray *gaucherie* of that kind."

Blanche Heriot doubted. She never supposed but that he whom she called father had her true interest at heart, and must be so acting. Mrs. Guy, too, unconsciously swayed her. A martyr to poverty herself, she believed that in marrying one so well-off as Captain Cross, a girl must enter upon the seventh heaven of happiness. Altogether, Blanche yielded; yielded against her inclination and her better judgment. She consented to marry Captain Cross, and preparations were begun.

Meanwhile, Arnold Ravensworth had been an occasional visitor at Major Carlen's, the Major making no sort of objection, now that circumstances were explained: indeed, he encouraged him there, and was especially cordial. Major Carlen had invariably one eye on the world and the other on self-interest, and it occurred to him that a rising man, as Arnold Ravensworth beyond doubt was, might prove useful to him in one way or another.

One evening, when it was yet only the beginning of April, Mr. Ravensworth called in Gloucester Place, and found the Major alone.

"Are Mrs. Guy and Blanche out?" he asked.

"They are upstairs with the dressmaker," replied the Major. "We sent to her to-day to spur on with Blanche's things, and she has come to-night for fresh orders."

"Is the marriage being hurried on, Major?"

"Time is creeping on, sir," was the gruff answer.

"Are they getting ahead with the settlements? When I saw you last week, you were in a way at the delay, and said lawyers had only been invented for one's torment."

"They got on, after that, and the deeds were ready and waiting for signature. But I dropped them a note yesterday to say they might burn them, as so much waste paper," returned the Major.

"Burn the settlements!" echoed Mr. Ravensworth.

The Major's eyes, that could look pleasant on occasion, glinted at his astonishment. "Those settlements are being replaced by heavier ones," he said. "Blanche does not marry Captain Cross. It's off. A more eligible offer has been made her, and Cross is dismissed."

Mr. Ravensworth doubted whether he heard aright. Major Carlen resumed. "And she was making herself miserable over it. She cannot endure Cross."

"What a disappointment for Cross! What a mortification! Will he accept his dismissal?"

"He will be obliged to accept it," returned the Major, pulling up his shirt-collar, which was always high enough for two. "He has no other choice left to him. A man does not die of love nowadays; or rush into an action for breach of promise, and become a laughing-stock at his club. Blanche marries Lord Level."

"Lord Level!" Mr. Ravensworth repeated in a curious accent.

"You look as though you doubted the information."

"I do not relish it, for your daughter's sake," replied Mr. Ravensworth. "She never can—can—like Lord Level."

"What's the matter with Lord Level? He may be approaching forty, but—"

Mr. Ravensworth laughed. "Not just yet, Major Carlen."

"Well, say he's thirty-four; thirty-three, if you like. Blanche, at twenty, needs guiding. And if he is not as rich as some peers, he is ten times richer than Cross. He met Blanche out, and came dangling here after her. I did not give a thought to it, for I did not look upon Level as a marrying man: he has been somewhat talked of in another line—"

"Yes," emphatically interrupted Mr. Ravensworth. "Well?"

"Well!" irritably returned the Major: "then there's so much the more credit due to him for settling down. When he found that Cross was really expecting to have Blanche, and that he might lose her altogether, he spoke up, and said he should like her himself."

"Does Blanche approve of the exchange?"

"She was rather inclined to kick at it," returned the Major, in his respectable phraseology, "and we had a few tears.—But if you ask questions in that sarcastic tone, sir, you don't deserve to be answered. Not that Blanche wanted to keep Cross; she acknowledged that she was only too thankful to be rid of him; but, about behaving dishonourably, as she called it. 'My dear,' said I, 'there's your absurd rusticity coming in again. You don't know the world. Such things are done in high life every day.' She believed me, and was reconciled. You look black as a thunder-cloud, Ravensworth. What right have you to do so, pray?"

"None in the world. I beg pardon. I was thinking of Blanche's happiness."

"You had better think of her good," retorted the Major. "She likes Level. I don't say she is yet in love with him: but she did not like Cross. Level is an attractive man, remember."

"Has been rather too much so," cynically retorted Mr. Ravensworth.

"Here she comes. I am going out; so you may offer your congratulations at leisure."

Major Carlen went away, and Blanche entered. She took her seat by the fire, and as Mr. Ravensworth gazed down upon her, a feeling of deep regret and pity came over him. Shame! thought he, to sacrifice her to Level. For in truth that nobleman's name was not in the best odour, and Arnold Ravensworth was a man of strict notions.

It has been asserted that some natures possess an affinity the one for the other; are irresistibly drawn together in the repose of full and perfect confidence. It is a mysterious affinity, not born of *love*: and it may be experienced by two men or women who have outlived even the remembrance of the passion. Had Blanche Heriot been offered to Arnold Ravensworth, he would have declined her, for he loved another, and she had as much idea of loving the man in the moon as of loving him. Nevertheless, that never-dying, unfathomable part of them, the spirit, was attracted, like finding like. Between such, there can be little reserve.

"What unexpected changes take place, Blanche!"

"Do not blame me," she replied, with a rising colour, her tone sinking to a whisper. "My father says it is right, and I obey him."

"I hope you like Lord Level?"

"Better than I liked someone else," was her answer, as she looked into the fire. "At first the—the change frightened me. It did not seem right, and it was so very sudden. But I am getting over that feeling now. Papa says he is very good."

Papa says he is very good! The old hypocrite of a Major! thought Mr. Ravensworth. But it was not his place to tell her that Lord Level had not been very good.

"Oh, Blanche!" he exclaimed, "I hope you will be happy! Is it to be soon?"

"Yes, they say so. As soon, I think, as the settlements can be ready. Papa sent to-day to hurry on my wedding things. Lord Level is going abroad immediately, and wishes to take me with him."

"They say so!" was his mental repetition. "This poor child, brought up in the innocence of her simple country home, more childish, more tractable and obedient, more inexperienced than are those of less years who have lived in the world, is as a puppet in their hands. But the awakening will come."

"You are going?" said Blanche, as he rose. "Will you not stay and take tea? Mrs. Guy will be down soon."

"Not this evening. Hark! here is the Major back again."

"I do not think it is papa's step," returned Blanche, bending her ear to listen.

It was not. As she spoke, the door was thrown open by the servant. "Lord Level."

Lord Level entered, and took the hand which Mr. Ravensworth released. Mr. Ravensworth looked full at the peer as he passed him: they were not acquainted. A handsome man, with a somewhat free expression—a countenance that Mr. Ravensworth took forthwith a prejudice against, perhaps unjustly. "Who's that, Blanche?" he heard him say as the servant closed the door.

Lord Level was a fine, powerful man, of good height and figure; his dark auburn hair was wavy and worn rather long, in accordance with the fashion of the day. His complexion was fair and fresh, and his features were good. Altogether he was what the Major had called him, an attractive man. Blanche Heriot had danced with him and he had danced with her; the one implies the other, you will say; and a liking for one another had sprung up. It may not have been love on either side as yet—but that is uncertain.

"How lovely!" exclaimed Blanche, as he held out to her a small bouquet of lilies-of-the-valley, and their sweet perfume caught her senses.

"I brought them for you," whispered Lord Level; and he bent his face nearer and took a silent kiss from her lips. It was the first time; and Blanche blushed consciously.

"You did not tell me who that was, Blanche."

"Arnold Ravensworth," she replied. "You have heard me speak of him."

"An ill-tempered looking man!"

"Do you think so? Well, yes, perhaps he did look cross to-night. He had been hearing about—about *us*—from papa; and I suppose it did not please him."

Archibald Baron Level drew himself up to his full height; his face assumed its haughtiest expression. "What business is it of his?" he asked. "Does he wish to aspire to you himself?"

"Oh, no, no; he is soon to be married. He is a man of strict honour, and I fear he thinks that papa—that I—that we have not behaved well to Captain Cross."

They were standing side by side on the hearth-rug, the fire-light playing on them and on Blanche's shrinking face. How miserably uncomfortable the subject of Captain Cross made her she could never tell.

"See here, Blanche," spoke Lord Level, after a pause. "I was given to understand by Major Carlen that when Captain Cross proposed for you, you refused him; that it was only by dint of pressure and persuasion that you consented to the engagement. Major Carlen told me that as the time went on you became so miserable under it, hating Captain Cross with a greater dislike day by day, that he had resolved before I spoke *to save you by breaking it off*. Was this the case, or not?"

"Yes, it was. It is true that I felt wretchedly miserable in the prospect of marrying Captain Cross. And oh, how I thank papa for having himself resolved to break it off! He did not tell me that."

"Because I have some honour of my own; and I would not take you sneakingly from Cross, or any other man. You must come to me above-board in all ways, Blanche, or not at all."

Blanche felt her heart beating. She turned to glance at him, fearing what he might mean.

"So that if there is anything behind the scenes which has been kept from me; that is, if it be not of your own good and free will that you marry me; if you gave up Captain Cross *liking* him, because—because—well, though I feel ashamed to suggest such a thing—because my rank may be somewhat higher than his, or for any other reason: why then matters had better be at an end between us. No harm will have been done, Blanche."

Blanche's face was drawn and white. "Do you mean that you wish to give me up?"

"*Wish* it! It would be the greatest pain I could ever know in life. My dear, have you failed to understand me? I want you; I want you to be my wife; but not at the sacrifice of my honour. If Captain Cross—"

Blanche broke down. "Oh, *don't* leave me to him!" she implored. "Of course, I could never, never marry him now; I would rather die. Indeed, I do not quite know what you mean. It was all just as you have been told by papa; there was nothing kept behind."

Lord Level pillowed her head upon his arm. "Blanche, my dear, it was you who invoked this," he whispered, "by talking of Mr. Ravensworth's reflection on you in his 'strict honour.' Be assured I would not leave you to Captain Cross unless compelled to do so, or to any other man."

Her tears were falling. Lord Level kissed them away.

"Shall I *buy* you, my love?—bind you to me with a golden fetter?" And, taking a small case from his waistcoat-pocket, he slipped upon her marriage finger a hoop of gold, studded with diamonds. His deep-gray eyes were strained upon her through their dark lashes—eyes which had done mischief in their day—and her hand was lingering in his.

"There, Blanche; you see I have bought you; you are my property now—my very own. And, my dear, the ring must be worn always as the keeper of the marriage-ring when you shall be my wife."

It was a most exquisite relief to her. Blanche liked him far better than she had liked Captain Cross. And as Lord Level pressed his last kiss upon her lips—for Mrs. Guy was heard approaching—Blanche could never be sure that she did not return it.

A few more interviews such as these, and the young lady would be in love with him heart and soul.

And it may as well be mentioned, ere the chapter quite closes, that Mr. Charles Strange was out of the way of all this plotting and planning and love-making. The whole of that spring he was over in Paris, watching a case involving English and French interests of importance, that was on before the French courts, and of which Brightman and Strange were the English solicitors.

CHAPTER VII
TRIED AT THE OLD BAILEY

OH, Mrs. Guy, he is coming, after all! He is indeed!"

Blanche Heriot's joyful tones, as she read the contents of a short letter brought in by the evening post, aroused old Mrs. Guy, who was dozing over her knitting one Tuesday evening in the May twilight.

"Eh? What, my dear? Who do you say is coming?"

"Tom. He says he must stretch a point for once. He cannot let anyone else give me away."

"The Major is to give you away, Blanche."

"I know he intended to do so if Tom failed me. But Tom is my brother."

"Well, well, child; settle it amongst yourselves. I don't see that it matters one way or the other. There's a knock at the door! Dear me! It must be Lord Level."

"Lord Level cannot be back again before to-morrow. He is at Marshdale, you know," dissented Blanche. "I think it may be Tom. I hope it is Tom. He says here he shall be in town as soon as his letter."

"Mr. Strange," announced a servant, throwing wide the drawing-room door.

Charles Strange had only that morning returned from Paris, having crossed by the night mail. The legal business on which he and Mr. Brightman were just now so much occupied, involving serious matters for a client who lived in Paris, had kept Charles over there nearly all the spring. Blanche ran to his arms. She looked upon him as her brother, quite as much as she looked upon Tom.

"And so, Blanche, we are to lose you," he said, when he had kissed her. "And within a day or two, I hear."

He knew very little of Blanche Heriot's approaching marriage, except that the bridegroom was Archibald, Lord Level. And that little he had heard from Mr. Brightman. Blanche did not write to him about it. She had written to tell him she was going to be married to Captain Cross: but when that marriage was summarily broken off by Major Carlen, Blanche felt a little ashamed, and did not send word to Charles.

"The day after to-morrow, at eleven o'clock in the morning," put in Mrs. Guy, in response to the last remark.

All his attention given to Blanche, Charles Strange really had not observed the old lady. He turned to regard her.

"You cannot have forgotten Mrs. Guy, Charles," said Blanche, noticing his doubtful look.

"I believe I had for the moment," he answered, in those pleasant, cordial tones that won him a way with everyone, as he went up and shook the old lady heartily by both hands. "I heard you were staying here, Mrs. Guy, but I had forgotten it."

They sat down—Blanche and Charles near the open window, Mrs. Guy not moving from her low easy-chair on the hearthrug—and began to talk of the wedding.

"Tom is really coming up to give me away," said Blanche, showing him Captain Heriot's short note. "It is *very* good of him, for he must be very busy: but Tom was always good. You are aware, Charles, I suppose, that the regiment is embarking for India? Major Carlen saw the announcement this morning in the *Times*."

At that moment Charles Strange saw, or fancied he saw, a warning look telegraphed to him by Mrs. Guy: and, placing it in conjunction with Blanche's words, he fancied he must know its meaning.

"Yes, I heard the regiment was ordered out," he answered shortly; and turned the subject. "Will Lord Level be here tonight, Blanche? I should like to see him."

"No," she replied. "He went yesterday to Marshdale House, his place in Surrey, and will not return until to-morrow. I think you will like him, Charles."

"I hope you do," replied Charles involuntarily. "That is the chief consideration, Blanche."

He looked at her meaningly as he spoke, and it brought a blush to her face. What a lovely face it was—fair and pure, its blue eyes haughty as of yore, its golden hair brilliant and abundant! She wore a simple evening dress of white muslin, and a blue sash, an inexpensive necklace of twisted blue beads on her neck, no bracelets at all on her arms. She looked what she really was—an inexperienced school-girl. Lord Level's engagement ring on her finger, with its flashing diamonds, was the only ornament of value she had about her.

In the momentary silence that ensued, Blanche left her seat and went to stand at the open window.

"Oh," she exclaimed, an instant later, "I do think this may be Tom! A cab has stopped here."

Charles Strange rose. Mrs. Guy lifted her finger, and he bent down to her. Blanche was still at the window.

"She does not know he has sold out," warningly breathed Mrs. Guy. "She knows nothing of his wild ways, or the fine market he has brought his eggs to, poor fellow. We have kept it from her."

Charles nodded; and the servant opened the door with another announcement.

"Captain Heriot." Blanche flew across the room and was locked in her brother's arms.

Poor Tom Heriot had indeed, as Mrs. Guy expressed it, with more force than elegance, brought his eggs to a fine market. It was some few months now since he sold out of the Army; and what he was doing and how he contrived to exist and flourish without money, his friends did not know. During the spring he had made his appearance in Paris to prefer an appeal for help to Charles, and Charles had answered it to the extent of his power.

Just as gay, just as light-hearted, just as *débonnaire* as ever was Tom Heriot. To see him and to hear him as he sat this evening with them in Gloucester Place, you might have thought him as free from care as an Eton boy—as flourishing as a duke-royal. Little blame to Blanche that she suspected nothing of the existing state of things.

When Charles rose to say "Good-night," Tom Heriot said it also, and they went away together.

"Charley, lad," said the latter, as the street-door closed behind them, "could you put me up at your place for two nights—until after this wedding is over?"

"To be sure I can. Leah will manage it."

"All right. I have sent a portmanteau there."

"You did not come up from Southampton to-day, Tom? Blanche thought you did."

"And I am much obliged to them for allowing her to think it. I would have staked my last five-pound note, if you'll believe me, Charley, that old

Carlen had not as much good feeling in him. I am vegetating in London; have been for some time, Blanche's letter was forwarded to me by a comrade who lets me use his address."

"And what are you doing in London?" asked Charles.

"Hiding my 'diminished head,' old fellow," answered Tom, with a laugh. No matter how serious the subject, he could not be serious over it.

"How much longer do you mean to stand here?" continued Charles—for the Captain (people still gave him his title) had not moved from the door.

"Till an empty cab goes by."

"We don't want a cab this fine night, Tom. Let us walk. Look how bright the moon is up there."

"Ay; my lady's especially bright tonight. Rather too much so for people who prefer the shade. How you stare, Charley! Fact is, I feel safer inside a cab just now than parading the open streets."

"Afraid of being taken for debt?" whispered Charles.

"Worse than that," said Tom laconically.

"Worse than that!" repeated Charles. "Why, what do you mean?"

"Oh, nothing," and Tom Heriot laughed again. "Except that I am in the deuce's own mess, and can't easily get out of it. There's a cab! Here, driver! In with you, Charley."

And on the following Thursday, when his sister's marriage with Lord Level took place, who so gay, who so free from care, who so attractive as Tom Heriot?—when giving her away. Lord Level had never before seen his future brother-in-law (or *half* brother-in-law, as the more correct term would be), and was agreeably taken with him. A random young fellow, no doubt, given to playing the mischief with his own prospects, but a thorough gentleman, and a very prepossessing one.

"And this is my other brother—I have always called him so," whispered Blanche to her newly-made husband, as she presented Charles Strange to him on their return from church to Gloucester Place. Lord Level shook hands heartily; and Charles, who had been prejudiced against his lordship, of whom tales were told, took rather a liking to the tall, fine man of commanding presence, of handsome face and easy, genial manners.

After the breakfast, to which very few guests were bidden, and at which Mrs. Guy presided, as well as her nerves permitted, at one end of the table and Major Carlen at the other, Lord and Lady Level departed for Dover on their way to the Continent.

And in less than a week after the wedding, poor Thomas Heriot, who could not do an unkind action, who never had been anyone's enemy in the whole world, and never would be anyone's, except his own, was taken into custody on a criminal charge.

The blow came upon Charles Strange as a clap of thunder. That Tom was in a mess of some kind he knew well; nay, in half a dozen messes most likely; but he never glanced at anything so terrible as this. Tom had fenced with his questions during the day or two he stayed in Essex Street, and laughed them off. What the precise charge was, Charles could not learn at the first moment. Some people said felony, some whispered forgery. By dint of much exertion and inquiry, he at last knew that it was connected with "Bills."

Certain bills had been put into circulation by Thomas Heriot, and there was something wrong about them. At least, about one of them; since it bore the signature of a man who had never seen the bill.

"I am as innocent of it as a child unborn," protested Thomas Heriot to Charles, more solemnly in earnest than he had ever been heard to speak. "True, I got the bills discounted: accommodation bills, you understand, and they were to have been provided for; but that any good name had been *forged* to one of them, I neither knew nor dreamt of."

"Yet you knew the good name was there?"

"But I thought it had been genuinely obtained."

This was at the first interview Charles held with him in prison. "Whence did you get the bills?" Charles continued.

"They were handed to me by Anstey. He is the true culprit in all this, Charles, and he is slinking out of it, and will get off scot-free. People warned me against the fellow; said he was making a cat's-paw of me; and by Jove it's true! I could not see it then, but my eyes are open now. He only made use of me for his own purposes. He had all, or nearly all, the money."

And this was just the truth of the business. The man Anstey, a gentleman once, but living by his wits for many years past, had got hold of light-headed, careless Tom Heriot, cajoled him of his friendship, and *used* him. Anstey escaped completely "scot-free," and Tom suffered.

Tom was guilty in the eyes of the law; and the law only takes cognizance of its own hard requirements. After examination, he was committed for trial. Charles Strange was nearly wild with distress; Mr. Brightman was much concerned; Arthur Lake (who was now called to the Bar) would have moved heaven and earth in the cause. Away went Charles to Mr. Serjeant

Stillingfar: and that renowned special pleader and good-hearted man threw his best energies into the cause.

All in vain. At the trial, which shortly came on at the Old Bailey, Mr. Serjeant Stillingfar exerted his quiet but most telling eloquence uselessly. He might as well have wasted it on the empty air. Though indeed it did effect something, causing the sentence pronounced upon the unfortunate prisoner to be more lenient than it otherwise would have been. Thomas Heriot was sentenced to be transported for seven years.

Transportation beyond the seas was still in force then. And Thomas Heriot, with a cargo of greater or lesser criminals, was shipped on board the transport *Vengeance*, to be conveyed to Botany Bay.

It seemed to have taken up such a little space of time! Very little, compared with the greatness of the trouble. June had hardly come in when Tom was first taken; and the *Vengeance* sailed the beginning of August.

If Mrs. Guy had lamented beforehand the market that poor Tom Heriot had "brought his eggs to," what did she think of it now?

One evening in October a nondescript sort of vehicle, the German makers of which could alone know the name, arrived at a small village not far from the banks of the Rhine, clattering into the yard of the only inn the place contained. A gentleman and lady descended from it, and a parley ensued with the hostess, more protracted than it might have been, in consequence of the travellers' imperfect German, and her own imperfect French. Could madame accommodate them for the night, was the substance of their demand.

"Well—yes," was madame's not very assured answer: "if they could put up with a small bedroom."

"How small?"

She opened the door of—it was certainly not a room, though it might be slightly larger than a boot-closet; madame called it a cabinet-de-toilette. It was on the ground-floor, looking into the yard, and contained a bed, into which one person might have crept, provided he bargained with himself not to turn; but two people, never. Three of her beds were taken up with a milor and miladi Anglais, and their attendants.

Mrs. Ravensworth—a young wife—turned to her husband, and spoke in English. "Arnold, what can we do? We cannot go on in the dark, with such roads as these."

"My love, I see only one thing for it: you must sleep here, and I must sit up."

Madame interrupted; it appeared she added a small stock of English to her other acquirements. "Oh, but dat meeseraable for monsieur: he steef in legs for morning."

"And stiff in arms too," laughed Arnold Ravensworth. "Do try and find us a larger bedroom."

"Perhaps the miladi Anglaise might give up one of her rooms for dis one," debated the hostess, bustling away to ask.

She returned, followed by an unmistakable Englishwoman, fine both in dress and speech. Was *she* the miladi? She talked enough for one: vowing she would never give up her room to promiscuous travellers, who prowled about with no *avant courier*, taking their own chance of rooms and beds; and casting, as she spoke, annihilating glances at the benighted wanderers.

"Is anything the matter, Timms?" inquired a gentle voice in the background.

Mr. Ravensworth turned round quickly, for its tones struck upon his remembrance. There stood Blanche, Lady Level; and their hands simultaneously met in surprise and pleasure.

"Oh, this is unexpected!" she exclaimed. "I never should have thought of seeing you in this remote place. Are you alone?"

He drew his wife to his side. "I need not say who she is, Lady Level."

"Are you married, then?"

"Ask Mary."

It was an unnecessary question, seeing her there with him, and Lady Level felt it to be so, and smiled. Timms came forward with an elaborate apology and a string of curtseys, and hoped her room would be found good enough to be honoured by any friends of my lady's.

Lady Level's delight at seeing them seemed as unrestrained as a child's. Exiles from their native land can alone tell that to meet with home faces in a remote spot is grateful as the long-denied water to the traveller in the Eastern desert. And we are writing of days when to travel abroad was the exception, rather than the rule. "There is only one private sitting-room in the whole house, and that is mine, so you must perforce make it yours as well," cried Lady Level, as she laughingly led the way to it. "And oh! what a charming break it will be to my loneliness! Last night I cried till bedtime."

"Is not Lord Level with you?" inquired Mr. Ravensworth.

"Lord Level is in England. While they are getting Timms' room ready, will you come into mine?" she added to Mrs. Ravensworth.

"How long have you been married?" was Lady Level's first question as they entered it.

"Only last Tuesday week."

"Are you happy?"

"Oh yes."

"I knew your husband long before you did," added Lady Level. "Did he ever tell you so? Did he ever tell you what good friends we were? Closer friends, I think, than he and his cousin Cecilia. He used to come to White Littleham Rectory, and we girls there made much of him."

"Yes, he has often told me."

Mrs. Ravensworth was arranging her hair at the glass, and Lady Level held the light for her and looked on. The description given of her by Blanche to her father was a very good one. A pale, gentle girl, with nice eyes, dark, inexpressively soft and attractive. "I shall like you very much," suddenly exclaimed Lady Level. "I think you are very pretty—I mean, you have the sort of face I like to look at." Praise that brought a blush to the cheeks of Mrs. Ravensworth.

The landlady sent them in the best supper she could command at the hour; mutton chops, served German fashion, and soup, which Lady Level's man-servant, Sanders, who waited on them, persisted in calling the potash—and very watery potash it was, flavoured with cabbage. When the meal was over, and the cloth removed, they drew round the fire.

"Do you ever see papa?" Lady Level inquired of Mr. Ravensworth.

"Now and then. Not often. He has let his house again in Gloucester Place, and Mrs. Guy has gone back to the Channel Islands."

"Oh yes, I know all that," replied Blanche.

"The last time I saw Major Carlen he spoke of you—said that you and Lord Level were making a protracted stay abroad."

"Protracted!" Blanche returned bitterly; "yes, it is protracted. I long to be back in England, with a longing that has now grown into a disease. You have heard of the *mal du pays* that sometimes attacks the Swiss when they are away from their native land; I think that same malady has attacked me."

"But why?" asked Mr. Ravensworth, looking at her.

"I hardly know," she said, with some hesitation. "I had never been out of England before, and everything was strange to me. We went to Switzerland first, then on to Italy, then back again. The longer we stayed away from England, the greater grew my yearning for it. In Savoy I was ill;

yes, I was indeed; we were at Chambéry; so ill as to require medical advice. It was on the mind, the doctor said. He was a nice old man, and told Lord Level that I was pining for my native country."

"Then, of course, you left for home at once?"

"We left soon, but we travelled like snails; halting days at one place, and days at another. Oh, I was so sick of it! And the places were all dull and retired, as this is; not those usually frequented by the English. At last we arrived here; to stay also, it appeared. When I asked why we did not go on, he said he was waiting for letters from home."

As Lady Level spoke she appeared to be lost in the past—an expression that you may have observed in old people when they are telling you tales of their youth. Her eyes were fixed on vacancy, and it was evident that she saw nothing of the objects around her, only the time gone by. She appeared to be anything but happy.

"Something up between my lord and my lady," thought Mr. Ravensworth. "Had your husband to wait long for the expected letters?" he asked aloud.

"I do not know: several came for him. One morning he had one that summoned him to England without the loss of a moment, and he said there was not time for me to be ready to accompany him. I prayed to go with him. I said Timms could come on afterwards with the luggage. It was of no use."

"Would he not take you?" exclaimed Mrs. Ravensworth, her eyes full of the astonishment her lips would not express.

Blanche shook her head. "No. He was quite angry with me; said I did not understand my position—that noblemen's wives could not travel in that unceremonious manner. I was on the point of telling him that I wished, to my heart, I had never been a nobleman's wife. Why did he marry me, unless he could look upon me as a companion and friend?" abruptly continued Lady Level, perhaps forgetting that she was not alone. "He treats me as a child."

What answer could be made to this?

"When do you expect him back again?" asked Mr. Ravensworth, after a pause.

"How do I know?" flashed Lady Level, her tone proving how inexpressibly sore was the subject. "He said he should return for me in a few days, but nearly three weeks have gone by, and I am still here. They have seemed to me like three months. I shall be ill if it goes on much longer."

"Of course you hear from him?"

"Oh yes, I hear from him. A few lines at a time, saying he will come for me as soon as he possibly can, and that I must not be impatient. I wanted to go over alone, and he returned me such an answer, asking what I meant by wishing to travel with servants only at my age. I shall do something desperate if I am left here another week."

"As you once did at White Littleham when they forbade your going to a concert, thinking you were too ill!" laughed Mr. Ravensworth.

"Dressed myself up in my best frock, and surprised them in the room. I had ten pages of Italian translation for that escapade."

"Do you like Italy?" he inquired, after a pause.

"No, I hate it!" And the animus in Lady Level's answer was so intense that the husband and wife exchanged stolen glances. *Something* must be out of gear.

"What parts of Italy did you stay in?"

"Chiefly at Pisa—that is not far from Florence, you know; and a few days at Florence. Lord Level took a villa at Pisa for a month—and why he did so I could not tell, for it was not the season when the English frequent it: no one, so to say, was there. We made the acquaintance of a Mrs. Page Reid, who had the next villa to ours."

"That was pleasant for you—if you liked her."

"But I did not like her," returned Lady Level, her delicate cheeks flushing. "That is, I did and I did not. She was a very pleasant woman, always ready to help us in any way; but she told dreadful tales of people—making one suspect things that otherwise would never have entered the imagination. Lord Level liked her at first, and ended by disliking her."

"Got up a flirtation with her," thought Mr. Ravensworth. But in that he was mistaken. And so they talked on.

It appeared that the mail passed through the village at night time; and the following morning a letter lay on the breakfast-table for Lady Level.

> My Dear Blanche,—I have met with a slight accident,
> and must again postpone coming to you for a few days.
> I dare say it will not detain me very long. Rely upon it
> I shall be with you as soon as I possibly can be.—Ever
> affectionately yours, Level.

"Short and sweet!" exclaimed Blanche, in her bitter disappointment, as she read the note at the window. "Arnold, when you and your wife leave to-morrow, what will become of me, alone here? If—"

Suddenly, as Lady Level spoke the last word, she started, and began to creep away from the window, as if fearing to be seen.

"Arnold! Arnold! who do you think is out there?" she exclaimed in a timid whisper.

"Why, who?" in astonishment. "Not Lord Level?"

"It is Captain Cross," she said with a shiver. "I would rather meet the whole world than him. My behaviour to him was—was not right; and I have felt ashamed of myself ever since."

Mr. Ravensworth looked out from the window. Captain Cross, seated on the bench in the inn yard, was solacing himself with a cigar.

"I would not meet him for the world! I would not let him see me: he might make a scene. I shall stay in my rooms all day. Why does my husband leave me to such chances as these?"

That Captain Cross had not been well used was certain; but the fault lay with Major Carlen, not with Blanche. Mr. Ravensworth spoke.

"Take my advice, Lady Level. Do not place yourself in Captain Cross's way, but do not run from him. I believe him to be a gentleman; and, if so, he will not say or do anything to annoy you. I will take care he does not, as long as I remain here."

In the course of the morning Captain Cross and Arnold Ravensworth met. "I find Lady Level's here!" the Captain abruptly exclaimed. "Are you staying with her?"

"I and my wife arrived here only last night, and were surprised to meet Lady Level."

"Where's *he*?" asked Captain Cross.

"In England."

"He in England and she here, and only six months married! Estranged, I suppose. Well, what else could she expect? People mostly reap what they sow."

Arnold Ravensworth laughed good-humouredly. *He* was not going to give a hint of the state of affairs that he suspected himself.

"You are prejudiced, Cross. Miss Heriot was not to blame for what happened. She was a child: and they did with her as they pleased."

"A child! Old enough to engage herself to one man, and to marry another," retorted Captain Cross, in a burst of angry feeling. "And Level, of all people!"—with sarcastic scorn. "Why does he leave her in Germany whilst he stays gallivanting in England? What do you say? Met with an accident, and *can't* come for her? That's *his* tale, I suppose. You may repeat it to the Marines, old boy; it won't do for me. *I* know Level; knew him of old."

Lady Level was as good as her word: she did not stir out of her rooms all day. On the following morning when Mr. Ravensworth came out of his chamber, he saw, from the corridor window, a travelling-carriage in the yard, packed. By the coat-of-arms he knew it for Lord Level's. Timms moved towards him in a flutter of delight.

"Oh, if you please, sir, breakfast is on the table, and my lady is waiting there, ready dressed. We are going to England, sir."

"Has Lord Level come?"

"No, sir: we are going with you. My lady gave orders, last night, to pack up for home. It is the happiest day I've known, sir, since I set foot in these barbarious countries."

Lady Level met him at the door of the breakfast-room; "ready dressed," as Timms expressed it, for travelling, even to her bonnet.

"Do you really mean to go with us?" he exclaimed.

"Yes," was her decisive reply. "That is, you must go with me. Stay here longer, I will not. I tell you, Arnold, I am sick to death of it. If Lord Level is ill and unable to come for me, I am glad to embrace the opportunity of travelling under your protection: he can't grumble at that. Besides—"

"Besides what?" asked Mr. Ravensworth, for she suddenly stopped.

"I do not choose to remain at an inn in which Captain Cross has taken up his abode: neither would my husband wish me to do so. After you and Mrs. Ravensworth left me last night, I sat over the wood fire, thinking these things over, and made my mind up. If I have not sufficient money for the journey, and I don't think I have, I must apply to you, Arnold."

Whether Mr. Ravensworth approved or disapproved of the decision, he had no power to alter it. Or, rather, whether Lord Level would approve of it. After a hasty breakfast, they went down to the carriage, which had already its array of five horses harnessed to it; Sanders and Timms perched side-by-side in their seat aloft. The two ladies were helped in by Mr. Ravensworth. Captain Cross leaned against the outer wall of the *salle-à-manger*, watching the departure. He approached Mr. Ravensworth.

"Am I driving her ladyship off?"

"Lady Level is going to England with us, to join her husband. I told you he had met with an accident."

"A merry meeting to them!" was the sarcastic rejoinder. And, as the carriage drove out of the inn-yard, Captain Cross deliberately lifted his hat to Lady Level: but lifted it, she thought, in mockery.

CHAPTER VIII
THE VINE-COVERED COTTAGE AT PISA

THAT Archibald, Lord Level, had been a gay man, fond of pleasure, fond of talking nonsense to pretty women, the world knew well: and perhaps, world-fashion, admired him none the less for it. But his wife did not know it. When Blanche Heriot became Blanche Level she was little more than an innocent child, entirely unversed in the world's false ways. She esteemed her husband; ay, and loved him, in a measure, and she was happy for a time.

It is true that while they were staying in Switzerland a longing for home came over her. They had halted in Paris for nearly a fortnight on their outward route. Some very nice people whom Lord Level knew were there; they were delighted with the fair young bride, and she was delighted with them. Blanche was taken about everywhere, no one being more anxious for her amusement than Lord Level himself. But one morning, in the very midst of numerous projected expeditions, he suddenly told Blanche that they must continue their journey that day.

"Oh, Archibald!" she had answered in a sort of dismay. "Why, it is this very afternoon that we were going to Fontainebleau!"

"My dear, you shall see Fontainebleau the next time we are in Paris," he said. "I have a reason for wishing to go on at once."

And they went on. Blanche was far too good and dutiful a wife to oppose her own will to her husband's, or to grumble. They went straight on to Switzerland—travelling in their own carriage—but instead of settling himself in one of those pretty dwellings on the banks of Geneva's lake, as he had talked of to Blanche, Lord Level avoided Geneva altogether, and chose a fearfully dull little village as their place of abode. Very lovely as to scenery, it is true; but quite unfrequented by travellers. It was there that Blanche first began to long for home.

Next, they went on to Italy, posting straight to Pisa, and there Lord Level took a pretty villa for a month in the suburbs of the town. Pisa itself was deserted: it was hot weather; and Blanche did not think it had many attractions. Lord Level, however, seemed to find pleasure in it. He knew Pisa well, having stayed at it in days gone by. He made Blanche familiar with the neighbourhood; together they admired and wondered at the Leaning Tower, in its green plain, backed by distant mountains; but he also went out and about a good deal alone.

One English dame of fashion was sojourning in the place—a widow, Mrs. Page Reid. She occupied the next villa to theirs, and called upon them; and she and Lady Level grew tolerably intimate. She was a talkative, gay woman of thirty—and beside her Blanche seemed like a timid schoolgirl.

One evening, when dinner was over, Lord Level strolled out—as he often did—leaving his wife with Mrs. Page Reid, who had dined with them. The two ladies talked together, and sang a song or two; and so whiled away the time.

"Let us go out for a stroll, too!" exclaimed Mrs. Page Reid, speaking on a momentary impulse, when she found the time growing monotonous.

Blanche readily agreed. It was a most lovely night; the moon bright and silvery in the Italian sky. Putting on some fleecy shawls, the ladies went down the solitary road, and turned by-and-by into a narrow lane that looked like a grove of evergreens. Soon they came to a pretty dwelling-place on the left, half villa, half cottage. Vines grew up its trellised walls, flowers and shrubs crowded around it.

"A charming little spot!" cried Mrs. Page Reid, as they halted to peep through the hedge of myrtles that clustered on each side the low entrance-gate. "And two people are sitting there—lovers, I dare say," she added, "telling their vows under the moonbeams."

In front of the vine-wreathed window, on a bench overhung by the branches of the trailing shrubs, the laurels and the myrtles, sat two young people. The girl was tall, slender, graceful; her dark eyes had a flashing fire even in the moonlight; her cheeks wore a rose-red flush.

"How pretty she is!" whispered Blanche. "Look at her long gold earrings! And he— Oh!"

"What's the matter?" cried Mrs. Page Reid, the tone of the last word startling her.

"It is my husband."

"Nonsense!" began Mrs. Page Reid. But after one doubting, disbelieving look, she saw that it was so. Catching Blanche's hand, she drew her forcibly away, and when they had gained the highroad, burst into a long, low laugh.

"Don't think about it, dear," she said to Blanche. "It's nothing. The best of husbands like to amuse themselves behind our backs."

"Perhaps he was—was—inquiring the way—or something," hazarded Blanche, whose breath was coming rather faster than usual.

Mrs. Page Reid nearly choked. "Oh, to be sure!" she cried, when she could speak.

"You don't think so? You think it was—something else?"

"You are only a little goose, my dear, in the ways of the world," rejoined Mrs. Page Reid. "Where's the man that does not like to talk with a pretty woman? Lord Level, of all others, does."

"*He* does?"

"Well, he used to do so. Of course he has mended his manners. And the women, mind you, liked to talk to him. But don't take up the notion, please, that by saying that I insinuate any unorthodox talking," added Mrs. Page Reid as an after-thought, when she caught a look at Lady Level's tell-tale countenance.

"I shall ask Lord Level—"

"*Ask nothing,*" impressively spoke the elder lady, cutting short the words. "Say nothing to your husband. Take my advice, Lady Level, for it is good. There is no mortal sin a wife can commit so repugnant in her husband's eyes as that of spying upon his actions. It would make him detest her in the end."

"But I was not spying. We saw it by accident."

"All the same. Let it pass from your mind as though it had never been."

Blanche was dubious. *If* there was no harm, why should she not speak of it?—and she could not think there was harm. And if there *was*—why, she would not have breathed it to him for the world. Dismissing the subject, she and Mrs. Page Reid sat down to a quiet game at cards. When Lord Level came in, their visitor said good-night.

Blanche sat on in silence and torment. Should she speak, or should she not? Lord Level seemed buried in a reverie.

"Archibald," she presently began.

"Yes," he answered, rousing himself.

"I—we—I and Mrs. Page Reid went out for a little walk in the moonlight. And—"

"Well, my dear?"

"We saw you," Blanche was wishing to say; but somehow her courage failed her. Her breath was short, her throat was beating.

"And it was very pleasant," she went on. "As warm and light as day."

"Just so," said Lord Level. "But the night air is treacherous, apt to bring fever. Do not go out again in it, love."

So her effort to speak had failed. And the silence only caused her to think the more. Blanche Level would have given her best diamond earrings to know who that person was in the gold ones.

An evening or two further on, when she was quite alone, Lord Level having again strolled out, she threw on the same fleecy shawl and betook herself down the road to the cottage in the grove—the cottage that looked like a pretty bower in the evergreens. And—yes—

Well, it was a strange thing—a startling thing; startling, anyway, to poor Blanche Level's heart; but there, on the self-same bench, side by side, sat Lord Level and the Italian girl. Her face looked more beautiful than before to the young wife's jealous eyes; the gold earrings glittered and sparkled in the moonlight. He and she were conversing in a low, earnest voice, and Lord Level was smoking a cigar.

Blanche stood rooted to the spot, shivering a little as she peered through the myrtle hedge, but never moving. Presently the young woman lifted her head, called out "Si," and went indoors, evidently in answer to a summons.

"Nina," sang out Lord Level. "Nina"—raising his voice higher—"I have left my cigar-case on the table; bring it to me when you come out again."

He spoke in English. The next minute the girl returned, cigar-case in hand. She took her place by his side, as before, and they fell to talking again.

Lady Level drew away. She went home with flagging steps and a bitterly rebellious heart.

Not to her husband would she speak; her haughty lips were sealed to him—and should be ever, she resolved in her new pain. But she gave a hint the next day of what she had again seen to Mrs. Page Reid.

That lady only laughed. To her mind it was altogether a rich joke. Not only the affair itself, but Blanche's ideas upon it.

"My dear Lady Level," she rejoined, "as I said before, you are very ignorant of the ways of the world. I assure you our husbands like to chatter to others as well as to us. Nothing wrong, of course, you understand; the mistake is, if we so misconstrue it. Lord Level is a very attractive man, you know, and has had all sorts of escapades."

"I never knew that he had had them."

"Well, it is hardly likely he would tell you of them before you were his wife. He will tell you fast enough some day."

"Won't you tell me some of them now?"

Blanche was speaking very equably, as if worldly wisdom had come to her all at once; and Mrs. Page Reid began to ransack her memory for this, that, or the other that she might have heard of Lord Level. As tales of scandal never lose by carrying, she probably converted mole-hills into mountains; most assuredly so to Blanche's mind. Anyway, she had better have held her tongue.

From that time, what with one doubt and another, Lady Level's regard for her lord was changed. Her feeling towards him became most bitter. Resentment?—indignation?—neither is an adequate word for it.

At the week's end they left Pisa, for the month was up, and travelled back by easy stages to Savoy. Blanche wanted to go direct to England, but Lord Level objected: he said she had not yet seen enough of Switzerland. It was in Savoy that her illness came on—the mal du pays, as they called it. When she grew better, they started towards home; travelling slowly and halting at every available spot. That his wife's manner had changed to him, Lord Level could only perceive, but he had no suspicion of its cause. He put it down to her anger at his keeping her so long away from England.

The morning after they arrived at the inn in Germany (of which mention has been made) Lord Level received a letter, which seemed to disturb him. It was forwarded to him by a banker in Paris, to whom at present all his letters were addressed. Telling Blanche that it contained news of some matter of business upon which he must start for London without delay, he departed; declining to listen to her prayer that she might accompany him, but promising to return for her shortly. It was at that inn that Arnold Ravensworth and his wife found Lady Level: and it was with them she journeyed to England.

And here we must give a few words to Lord Level himself. He crossed the Channel by the night mail to Dover, and reached London soon after daybreak. In the course of the day he called at his bankers', Messrs. Coutts and Co., to inquire for letters: orders having now been given by him to Paris to forward them to London. One only awaited him, which had only just then come in.

As Lord Level read it, he gave utterance to a word of vexation. For it told him that the matter of business upon which he had hurried over was put off for a week: and he found that he might just as well have remained in Germany.

The first thought that crossed his mind was—should he return to his wife? But it was hardly worth while doing so. So he took rooms in Holles Street, at a comfortable house where he had lodged before, and looked up friends and acquaintances at his club. But he did not let that first day pass without calling on Charles Strange.

The afternoon was drawing to an end in Essex Street, and Charles was in his own private room, all his faculties given to a deed, when Lord Level was shown in. It was for Charles he asked, not for Mr. Brightman.

"What an awful business this is!" began his lordship, when greetings had passed.

Charles lifted his hands in dismay. No need to ask to whom the remark applied: or to mention poor Tom Heriot by name.

"Could *nothing* be done, Mr. Strange?" demanded the peer in his coldest and haughtiest tones. "Were there *no* means that could have been taken to avert exposure?"

"Yes, I think there might have been, but for Tom's own careless folly: and that's the most galling part of it," returned Charles. "Had he only made a confidant of me beforehand, we should have had a try for it. If I could not have found the money myself, Mr. Brightman would have done so."

"You need only have applied to me," said Lord Level. "I should not have cared how much I paid—to prevent exposure."

"But in his carelessness, you see, he never applied to anyone; he allowed the blow to fall upon him, and then it was too late—"

"Was he a fool?" interjected Lord Level.

"There is this excuse for his not speaking: he did not know that things were so bad, or that the people would proceed to extremities."

The peer drew in his haughty lips. "Did he tell you that pretty fable?"

"Believe this much, Lord Level: what Tom *said*, he *thought*. Anyone more reprehensibly light and heedless I do not know, but he is incapable of falsehood. And in saying that he did not expect so grave a charge, or believe there were any grounds on which it could be made, I am sure he spoke only the truth. He was drawn in by one Anstey, and—"

"I read the reports of the trial," interrupted Lord Level. "Do not be at the pain of going over the details again."

"Well, the true culprit was Anstey; there's no doubt of that. But, like most cunning rogues, he was able to escape consequences himself, and throw them upon Tom. I am sure, Lord Level, that Tom Heriot no more knew the bill was forged than I knew it. He knew well enough there was something shady about it; about that and others which had been previously in circulation, and had been met when they came to maturity. This one bill was different. Of course there's all the difference between shady bills of accommodation, and a bill that has a responsible man's name to it, which he never signed himself."

"But what on earth possessed Heriot to allow himself to be drawn into such toils?"

"Ah, there it is. His carelessness. He has been reprehensibly careless all his life. And now he has paid for it. All's over."

"He is already on his passage out in the convict ship *Vengeance,* is he not?" said Lord Level, with suppressed rage.

"Yes: ever since early in August," shuddered Charles. "How does Blanche bear it?"

"Blanche does not know it."

"Not know it!"

"No. As yet I have managed to keep it from her. I dread its reaching her, and that's the truth. It is a fearful disgrace. She is fond of him, and would feel it keenly."

"But I cannot understand how it can have been kept from her."

"Well, it has been. Why, she does not even know that he sold out! She thinks he embarked with the regiment for India last May! We had been in Paris about ten days—after our marriage, you know—when one morning, happening to take up the *Times*, I saw in it the account of his apprehension and first examination. They had his name in as large as life—Thomas Heriot. 'Some gross calumny,' I thought; 'Blanche must not hear of this:' and I gave orders for continuing our journey that same day. However, I soon found that it was not a calumny: other examinations took place, and he was committed for trial. I kept my wife away from all places likely to be frequented by the English, lest a word should be dropped to her: and as yet, as I tell you, she knows nothing of it. She is very angry with me in her heart, I can see, for taking her to secluded places, and for keeping her away from England so long, but this has been my sole motive. I want the thought of it to die out of people's minds before I bring her home."

"She is not with you, then?"

"She is in Germany. I had to hasten over here upon a matter of business, and shall return for her when it is finished. I have taken my old rooms in Holles Street for a week. You must look me up there."

"I will," said Charles.

Mr. Brightman came in then, and the trouble was gone over again. Lord Level felt it keenly; there could be no doubt of that. He inquired of the older and more experienced lawyer whether there was any chance of bringing Anstey to a reckoning, so that he might be punished; and as to any expense, great or small, that might be incurred in the process, his lordship added, he would give carte blanche for that with greater delight than he had given money for anything in his whole life.

Charles could not help liking him. With all his pride and his imputed faults, few people could help liking Lord Level.

Meanwhile, as may have been gathered in the last chapter, Lord Level was detained in England longer than he had thought for. Lady Level grew impatient and more impatient at the delay: and then, taking the reins into her own hands, she crossed the Channel with Mr. and Mrs. Arnold Ravensworth.

CHAPTER IX
COMPLICATIONS

CROSSING by the night boat from Calais, the travellers reached Dover at a very early hours of the morning. Lady Level, with her servants, proceeded at once to London; but Mrs. Ravensworth, who had been exceedingly ill on the passage, required some repose, and she and her husband waited for a later train.

"Make use of our house, Lady Level," said Mr. Ravensworth—speaking of his new abode in Portland Place. "The servants are expecting me and their mistress, and will have all things in readiness, and make you comfortable."

"Thank you all the same, Arnold," said Lady Level; "but I shall drive straight to my husband's rooms in Holles Street."

"I would not—if I were you," he dissented. "You are not expected, and may not find anything ready in lodgings, so early in the morning. Drive first to my house and have some breakfast. You can go on to Holles Street afterwards."

Sensible advice. And Lady Level took it.

In the evening of that same day, Arnold Ravensworth and his wife reached Portland Place from the London terminus. To Mr. Ravensworth's surprise, who should be swinging from the door as the cab stopped but Major Carlen in his favourite purple and scarlet cloak, his gray hair disordered and his eyes exceeding fierce.

"Here's a pretty kettle-of-fish!" cried he, scarcely giving Arnold time to hand out his wife, and following him into the hall. "*You* have done a nice thing!"

"What is amiss?" asked Mr. Ravensworth, as he took the Major into a sitting-room.

"Amiss!" returned the excited Major. "I would advise you not to fall into Level's way just now. How the mischief came you to bring Blanche over?"

"We accompanied Lady Level to England at her request: I took no part in influencing her decision. Lady Level is her own mistress."

"Is she, though! She'll find she's not, if she begins to act in opposition to her husband. Before she was married, she had not a wish of her own, let alone a will—and there's where Level was caught, I fancy," added the Major, in a parenthesis, nodding his head knowingly. "He thought he had picked up a docile child, who would never be in his way. What with that and her beauty—anyway, he could not think she would be setting up a will, and an obstinate one, as she's doing now, rely upon that."

Major Carlen was striding from one end of the room to the other, his cloak catching in the furniture as he swayed about. Arnold thought he had been drinking: but he was a man who could take a great deal, and show it very little.

"The case is this," said he, unfastening the troublesome cloak, and flinging it on to a chair. "Level has been in England a week or two; amusing himself, I take it. He didn't want his wife, I suppose; well and good: men like a little society, and as long as they keep their wives in the dark, there's no reason why they shouldn't have it—"

"Major Carlen!" burst forth Mr. Ravensworth. "Lord Level's wife is your daughter. Have you forgotten it?"

"My step-daughter. What if she is? Does that render her different from others? Are you going to climb a pole and cry Morality? You are a young married man, Arnold Ravensworth, and must be on your good behaviour just now; it's etiquette."

Mr. Ravensworth was not easily excited, but the red flush of anger darkened his cheek. He could have thrust the old rascal from the house.

"Level leaves his wife in France, and tells her to remain there. Germany? Well, say Germany, then. My lady chooses to disobey, and comes to England, under your wing: and I wish old Harry had driven you to any place rather than the one she was stopping at. She reaches town to-day, and drives to Lord Level's rooms in Holles Street, whence he had dated his letters to her—and a model of incaution he was for doing it; why couldn't he have dated from his club? My lady finds or hears of something there she does not like. Well, what could she expect? They were his rooms; taken for himself, not for her; and if she had not been a greater simpleton than ever broke loose from keeping, she would have come away, then and there. Not she. She must persist in putting questions as to this and that; so at last she learned the truth, I suppose, or something near it. Then she thought it time to leave the house and come to mine: which is what she ought to have done at first: and there she has been waiting until now to see me, for I have been out all day."

"I thought your house was let?"

"It was let for the season; the people have left it now. I came home only yesterday from Jersey. My sister is lying ill there."

"And may I ask, Major Carlen, how you know that Lord Level has been 'amusing himself' if you have not been here to see?" questioned Mr. Ravensworth sarcastically.

"How do I know it?—why, common sense tells me," stormed the Major. "I have not heard a word about Level, except what Blanche says."

"Is he in Holles Street?"

"Not now. He gave up the rooms a week ago, and went down to Marshdale, his place in Surrey. He is laid up there, having managed to jam his knee against a gatepost; his horse swerved in going through it. A man I met to day, a friend of Level's, told me so. To go back to Blanche. She opened out an indignant tale to me, when I got home just now and found her there, of what she had heard in Holles Street. 'Serve you right, my dear,' I said to her: 'a wife has no business to be looking at her husband through a telescope. If a man chose to fill his rooms with wild tigers, it would not be his wife's province to complain, provided he kept her out of reach of their claws.' 'But what am I to do?' cried Blanche. 'You must return to France, or wherever else you came from,' I answered. 'That I never will: I shall go down to Marshdale, to Lord Level,' asserted Blanche, looking as I had never seen her look before. 'You can't go there,' I said: 'you must not attempt it.' 'I tell you, papa, I will go,' she cried, her eyes flashing. I never knew she had so much passion in her, Ravensworth: Level must have changed her nature. 'I will have an explanation from Lord Level,' she continued. 'Rather than live on as I am living now, I will demand a separation.'—Now, did you put that into her head?" broke off the Major, looking at Mr. Ravensworth.

"I do not think you know what you are saying, Major Carlen. Should I be likely to advise Lady Level to separate from her husband?"

"Someone has; such an idea would never enter Blanche's head unless put there. 'You must lend me the means to go down,' she went on. 'I am quite without money, through paying the bill at the hotel: Mr. Ravensworth had partly to supply my travelling expenses.' 'Then more fool Ravensworth for doing it,' said I; and more fool you were," repeated the Major.

"Anything more, Major?"

"The idea of my lending her money to take her down to Marshdale! And she'd be cunning to get money from me, just now, for I am out at all pockets. The last supplies I had came from Level; I wrote to him when he was abroad. By Jove! I would not cross him now for the universe."

"The selfish old sinner!" thought Mr. Ravensworth—and nearly said so aloud.

"Let me finish; she'll be here in a minute; she said she should come and apply to you. 'Does your husband beat you, or ill-treat you?' I asked her. 'No,' said she, shaking her head in a proud fury; 'even I would not submit to that. Will you lend me some money, papa?' she asked again. 'No, I won't,' I said. 'Then I'll borrow it from Mr. Ravensworth,' she cried, and ran upstairs to put her bonnet on. So then I thought it was time to come too, and explain. Mind you don't supply her with any, Ravensworth."

"What pretext can I have for refusing?"

"Pretext be shot!" irritably returned the Major. "Tell her you won't, as I do. I forbid you to lend her any. There she is! What a passionate knock! Been blundering up wrong turnings, I dare say."

Lady Level came in, looking tired, heated, frightened. Mr. Ravensworth took her hand.

"You have been walking here!" he said. "It is not right that Lady Level should be abroad in London streets at night, and alone."

"What else am I to do without money?" she returned hysterically.

"I sent the servants and the luggage to an hotel this morning, and gave them the few shillings I had left."

"Do sit down and calm yourself. All this is truly distressing."

Calm herself! The emotion, so long pent up, broke forth into sobs. "Yes, it is distressing. I come to England and I find no home; I am driven about from pillar to post, insulted everywhere; I have to walk through the streets, like any poor, helpless girl. Is it right that it should be so?"

"You have brought it all upon yourself, my lady," cried Major Carlen, coming forward from a dark corner.

She turned with a start. "So you are here, papa! Then I hope you have entered into sufficient explanation to spare it to me."

"I have told Ravensworth of your fine exploit, in going to Lord Level's rooms: and he agrees with me that no one except an inexperienced child would have done it."

"The truth, if you please, Major Carlen," struck in Mr. Ravensworth.

"And that what you heard or met with—though as to what it was I'm sure I'm all in a fog about—served you right for going," continued the unabashed Major.

Lady Level threw back her head, the haughty crimson dyeing her cheeks. "I went there expecting to find my husband; was that an inexperienced or a childish action?"

"Yes, it was," roared the Major, completely losing his temper, and showing his fierce teeth. "When men are away from their wives, they fall back into bachelor habits. If they please to turn their sanctums into smoking dens, or boxing dens, or what not, are you to come hunting them up, as I say, with a spyglass that magnifies at both ends?"

"Good men have no need to keep their wives away from them."

The Major gave his nose a twist. "Good men?—bad men?—where's the difference? The good have their wives under their thumb, and the bad haven't, that's all."

"For shame, papa!"

"Tie Lord Level to your apron-string, and keep him there as long as you can," fired the Major; "but don't ferret him up when he is out for a holiday."

"Did I want to ferret up Lord Level?" she retorted. "I went there because I thought it was his temporary home and would be mine. Why did he date his letters thence?"

"There it all lies," cried the Major, changing his tone to one of wrath against the peer. "Better he had dated from the top of the Monument. It is surprising what mistakes men make sometimes. But how was he to think you would come over against his expressed will? You say he had bade you stop there until he could fetch you."

Lady Level would not reply: the respect due to Major Carlen as her step-father was not in the ascendant just then. Turning to Mr. Ravensworth, she requested the loan of sufficient funds to take her down to Marshdale.

"I tell you, Blanche, you must not go there," interrupted the Major. "Better not. Lord Level does not receive strangers at Marshdale."

"Strangers!" emphatically repeated Lady Level.

"Or wives either. They are the same as strangers in a case such as this. I assure you Level told me, long before he married you, that Marshdale was a little secluded place, no establishment kept up in it, except an old servant or two; that he never received company down there, and should never take you to it. Remain at the hotel with your servants, if you will not come to my house, Blanche—there's only a charwoman in it at present, as you know. Then write to Level and let him know that you are there."

"Lady Level had better stay here tonight, at all events," put in Arnold Ravensworth. "My wife is expecting her to do so."

"Ay," acquiesced the old Major: "and write to Marshdale tomorrow, Blanche."

"I go down to Marshdale tomorrow," she replied in tones of determination. "It is too late to go tonight. The old servants that wait upon Lord Level can wait upon me: and if there are none, I will wait upon him myself. Go there I will, and have an understanding. And, unless Lord Level can explain away the aspect that things have taken, I—I—I—"

"Of all the imbeciles that ever gave utterance to folly, you are the worst," was the Major's complimentary retort, when she broke down. "Madam, do you know that you are a peeress of the realm?" he added pompously.

"I do not forget it."

"And you would stand in your own light! You have carriages and finery; you are to be presented next season; you will then have a house in town: what does the earth contain more that you *can* want?"

"Happiness," said Lady Level.

"Happiness!" repeated the Major, in genuine astonishment. "A pity but you had married a country curate and found it, then. Arnold Ravensworth, you must not lend Lady Level the money she desires; you shall not speed her on this insane journey."

Mr. Ravensworth approached him, and spoke in low tones. "Do you know of any existing reason that may render it inexpedient for her to go there?"

"I know nothing about it," replied the Major, too angry to lower his voice; "absolutely nothing. The Queen and all the princesses might pay it a visit, for aught I know of any reason to the contrary. But it is not Lady Level's place to follow her husband about in this clandestine manner. If he wants her there, he will send for her, once he knows that she is in London. The place is not much more than a farm, I believe, and used to be a hunting-box in the late Lord Level's time."

"Papa, I hope you will forgive me for running counter to your advice—but I shall certainly go down into Surrey tomorrow."

"I wash my hands of it altogether," said the angry Major.

"And you must lend me the money, Arnold."

"I will not refuse you," was his answer: "and I cannot dictate to you; but I think it would be better for you to remain here, and let Lord Level know that you are coming."

Lady Level shook her head. "Good advice, Arnold, no doubt, and I thank you; all the same, I shall go down as I have said."

"You will be very much to blame, sir, if you help on this mad scheme by so much as a sixpence," spoke the Major.

"Papa, listen to a word of common sense," she interposed. "I could go to a dozen places tomorrow, and get any amount of money. I could go to Lord Level's agents, and say I am Lady Level, and they would supply me. I could go to Mr. Brightman, and he would supply me—Charles Strange is in Paris again. I could go to other places. But I prefer to have it from Mr. Ravensworth, and save myself trouble and annoyance. It is not a pleasant thing for a peeress of the realm—as you just now put it—to go about borrowing a five-pound note," she concluded with a faint smile.

"Very well, Blanche. If ill comes of this wild step of yours, remember you were warned against it. I can say no more."

Gathering up his cloak as he spoke, Major Carlen threw it over his shoulders, and went forth, muttering, into the night.

Mr. Ravensworth called his wife, and she took Lady Level upstairs to a hastily-prepared chamber. Sitting down in a low chair, and throwing off her bonnet, Lady Level, worn out with all the excitement she had gone through, burst into a flood of hysterical tears.

"Tell me all about it," said Mary Ravensworth soothingly, drawing the poor wearied head to rest on her shoulder.

"They meant to stop me from going down to my husband, and I *will* go," sobbed Blanche half defiantly. "If he has met with an accident, and is ill, I ought to be there."

"Of course you ought," said Mary warmly. "But what is all the trouble about?—And what was it that you heard, and did not like, in Holles Street?"

"Oh, never mind that," said Blanche, colouring furiously. "That is what I am going to ask my husband to explain."

Upon Lady Level's arrival in London that morning, she sent her servants and luggage to an hotel, and drove straight to Portland Place herself: where Mr. and Mrs. Ravensworth's servants supplied her with breakfast. Afterwards, she went to Holles Street, arriving there about ten o'clock; walked into the passage, for the house door was open, was met by a young person in green, and inquired for Lord Level.

"Lord Level's not here now, ma'am," was the answer, as she showed Blanche into a parlour. "He has been gone about a week."

"Gone about a week!" repeated Blanche, completely taken back; for she had pictured him as lying at the place disabled.

"About that time, ma'am. He and the lady left together."

Blanche stared, and collected her scattered senses. "What lady?" she asked.

The young person in green considered. "Well, ma'am, I forget the name just now; those foreign names are hard to remember. His lordship called her Nina. A very handsome lady, she was—Italian, I think—with long gold earrings."

Lady Level's heart began to beat loudly. "May I ask if you are Mrs. Pratt?" she inquired, knowing that to be the name of the landlady.

"Dear me, no, ma'am; Mrs. Pratt's my aunt; I'm up here on a visit to her from the country. She is gone out to do her marketings. Lord Level was going down to his seat in Surrey, we understood, when he left here."

"Was the Italian lady going with him?"

The country girl—who was no doubt an inexperienced, simple country maiden, or she might not have talked so freely—shook her head. "We don't know anything about that, ma'am: she might have been. She was related to my lord—his sister-in-law, I think he called her to Mrs. Pratt—or some relation of that sort."

Blanche walked to the window and stood still for a moment, looking into the street, getting up her breath. "Did the lady stay with Lord Level all the time he was here?" she questioned, presently.

"Oh no, ma'am; she came only the day before he went away. Or, stay—the day but one before, I think it was. Yes; for I know they were out together nearly all the intervening day. Mrs. Pratt thought at his lordship's solicitor's. It was about six o'clock in the evening when she first arrived. My lord had spoken to Mrs. Pratt that day in his drawing-room, saying he was expecting a relative from Italy for a day or two, and could we let her have a bedroom, and any other accommodation she might need; and Mrs. Pratt said she would, for we were not full. A very nice lady she seemed to be, ma'am, and spoke English in a very pretty manner."

Lady Level drew in her contemptuous lips. "Did Lord Level meet with any accident while he was here?"

"Accident, ma'am! Not that we heard of. He was quite well when he left."

"Thank you," said Blanche, turning away and drawing her mantle up with a shiver. "As Lord Level is not here, I will not intrude upon you further."

Wishing the young person in green good-morning, she went away to Gloucester Place, feeling that she must scream or cry or fight the air. Blanche knew Major Carlen was about due in London, as his house was vacant again. Yes, the old charwoman said, the Major had got home the previous day, but he had just gone out. Would my lady (for she knew Blanche) like to walk in and wait until he returned?

My lady did so, and had to wait until evening. Then she partly explained to Major Carlen, and partly confused him; causing that gentleman to take up all kinds of free and easy ideas, as to the morals and manners of my Lord Level.

On the following morning Lady Level, pursuing her own sweet will, took train for Marshdale, leaving her servants behind her.

CHAPTER X
THE HOUSE AT MARSHDALE

IT was a gloomy day, not far off the gloomy month of November, and it was growing towards mid-day, when a train on a small line, branching from the direct London line, drew up at the somewhat insignificant station of Upper Marshdale. A young and beautiful lady, without attendants, descended from a first-class carriage.

"Any luggage, ma'am?" inquired a porter, stepping up to her.

"A small black bag; nothing else."

The bag was found in the van, and placed on the platform. A family, who also appeared to have arrived at their destination, closed round the van and were tumultuous over a missing trunk, and the lady drew back and accosted a stolid-looking lad, dressed in the railway uniform.

"How far is it to Marshdale?"

"Marshdale! Why, you be at Marshdale," returned the boy, in sulky tones.

"I mean Marshdale House."

"Marshdale House?—That be my Lord Level's place," said the boy, still more sulkily. "It be a matter of two mile."

"Are there any carriages to be hired?"

"There's one—a fly; he waits here when the train comes in."

"Where is it to be found?"

"It stands in the road, yonder. But if ye wants the fly, it's of no use wanting. It have been booked by them folks squabbling over their boxes: they writed here yesterday for it to be ready for 'em."

The more civil porter now came up, and the lady appealed to him. He confirmed the information that there was only this one conveyance to be had, and the family had secured it. Perhaps, he added, the lady might like to wait until they had done with it.

The lady shook her head impatiently, and decided to walk. "Can you come with me to carry my bag and to show me the way?" she asked of the surly boy.

The surly boy, willing or unwilling, had to acquiesce, and they set off to walk. Upon emerging from the station, he came to a standstill.

"Now, which way d'you mean to go?" began he, facing round upon his companion. "There's the road way, and it's plaguy long; two mile, good; and there's the field way, and it's a sight nearer."

"Is it as good as the road?"

"It's gooder—barring the bull. He runs at everybody. And he tosses 'em, if he can catch 'em."

Not caring to encounter so objectionable an animal, the lady chose the road; and the boy strode on before her, bag in hand. It was downhill all the way. In due time they reached Marshdale House, which lay in a hollow. It was a low, straggling, irregular structure, built of dark red brick, with wings and gable ends, and must originally have looked more like a comfortable farm-house than a nobleman's seat. But it had been added to at various periods, without any regard to outward appearance or internal regularity. It was exceedingly retired, and a very large garden surrounded the house, encompassed by high walls and dense trees.

The walls were separated by a pair of handsome iron gates, and a small doorway stood beside them. A short, straight avenue, overhung by trees, led to the front entrance of the house. The surly boy, turning himself and his bag round, pushed backwards against the small door, sent it flying, and branched off into a side-path.

"Is not that the front-door?" said the lady, trying to arrest him.

"'Tain't no manner of use going to it," replied the imperturbable boy, marching on. "The old gentleman and lady gets out o' the way, and the maids in the kitchen be deaf, I think. Last time I came up here with a parcel, I rung at it till I was tired, and nobody heard."

He went up to a side-door, flung it open, and put down the bag. A neat-looking young woman, with her sleeves turned up, came forward, and stared in silence.

"Is Lord Level within?" inquired the lady.

"My lord's ill in bed," replied the servant; "he cannot be seen or spoken to. What do you want with him, please?"

She seemed a good-tempered, ignorant sort of girl, but nothing more. At that moment someone called to her from an inner room, and she turned away.

"Are there not any upper servants in the house, do you know?" inquired the lady of the boy.

"I doesn't think so. There's the missis."

A tinge came over the lady's face. "The mistress! Who is she?"

"She's Mrs. Ed'ards. An old lady, what comes to church with buckles in her shoes. And there's Mr.—"

"What is it that you want here?" interrupted the servant girl, advancing again, and addressing the visitor in a not very conciliatory tone.

"I am Lady Level," was the reply, in a ringing, imperious voice. "Call someone to receive me."

It found its way to the girl's alarm. She looked scared, doubting, and finally turned and flew off down a long, dark passage. The boy heard the announcement without its ruffling his equanimity in the least degree.

"That's all, ain't it?" asked he, giving the bag a condescending touch with his foot.

"How much am I to pay you?" inquired Lady Level.

The boy paused. "You bain't obliged to pay nothing."

"What is the charge?" repeated Lady Level.

"The charge ain't nothing. If folks like to give anything, it's gived as a gift."

She smiled, and, taking out her purse, gave him half-a-crown. He received it with remarkable satisfaction, and then, with an air of great mystery and cunning, slipped it into his boot.

"But, I say, don't you go and tell, over there, as you gived it me," said he, jerking his head in the direction of the railway station. "We are not let take nothing, and there'd be the whole lot of 'em about my ears. You won't tell?"

"No, I will not tell," replied Lady Level, laughing, in spite of her cares and annoyances. And the promising young porter in embryo, giving vent to a shrill whistle, which might have been heard at the two-mile-off station, tore away as fast as his legs would carry him.

The girl came back with a quaint old lady. Her hair was white, her complexion clear and fresh, and her eyes were black and piercing as ever they had been in her youth. She looked in doubt at the visitor, as the servant had done.

"I am told that someone is inquiring for my lord."

"His wife is inquiring for him. I am Lady Level."

Had any doubt been wavering in the old lady's mind, the tones dispelled it. She curtseyed to the ground—the stately, upright, old-fashioned curtsey of the days gone by. A look of distress rose to her face.

"Oh, my lady! That I should live to receive my lord's wife in this unprepared, unceremonious manner! He told me you were in foreign parts, beyond seas."

"I returned to England yesterday, and have left my servants in town. What is the matter with Lord Level?"

"That your ladyship should come to such a house as this, all unfurnished and disordered! and—I beg your pardon, my lady! I cannot take you through these passages," she added, curtseying for Lady Level to go out again. "Deborah, go round and open the front-door."

Lady Level, in the midst of much lamentation, was conducted to the front entrance, and thence ushered into a long, low, uncarpeted room on the left of the dark hall. It was very bare of furniture, chairs and a large table being all that it contained. "It is of no consequence," said Lady Level; "I have come only to see Lord Level, and may not remain above an hour or two. I cannot tell. You are Mrs. Edwards, I think. I have heard Lord Level mention you."

"My name is Edwards, my lady. I was housekeeper in the late lord's time, and, when a young woman, I had the honour of nursing my lord. Since the late lord's death, I and my brother, Jacob Drewitt, have mostly lived here. He used to be house steward at Marshdale."

Lady Level removed her bonnet and cloak, and threw them on the table. She looked impatient and restless, as she listened to the account of her husband's accident. He had received an injury to his knee, when out riding, the day after his arrival at Marshdale; fever had set in, deepening at times to slight delirium.

"I should like to see him," said Lady Level. "Will you take me to his chamber?"

Mrs. Edwards marshalled her upstairs. Curious, in-and-out, wide and shallow stairs they were, with long passages and short turnings branching from them. She gently threw open the door of a large, handsome room. On the bed lay Lord Level, his eyes closed.

"He is dozing again, my lady," she whispered. "He is sure to fall to sleep whenever the fever leaves him."

"There is no fire in the room!" exclaimed Lady Level.

"The doctor says there's not to be any, my lady. In the room opposite to this, across the passage, you will find a good one. It is my lord's sitting-room when he is well. And here," noiselessly opening a door facing the foot of the bed, "is another chamber, that can be prepared for your ladyship, if you remain."

The housekeeper left the room as she spoke, scarcely knowing whether she stood on her head or her heels, so completely was she confounded by this arrival of Lady Level's—and nothing wherewith to receive her! Mrs. Edwards had her head and hands full just then.

As Lady Level moved forward, her dress came into contact with a light chair, and moved it. The invalid started, and raised himself on his elbow.

"Why!—who—is it?"

"It is I, Lord Level," she said, advancing to the bed.

He looked strangely amazed and perplexed. He could not believe his own eyes, and stared at her as though he would discover whether she was really before him, or whether he was in a dream.

"Don't you know me?" she asked gently.

"Is it—Blanche?"

"Yes."

"But where have you come from?—what brings you here?" he slowly ejaculated.

"I came down by train to-day. I have come to speak to you."

"You were in Germany. I left you in Germany!"

"I thought I had been there long enough: too long; and I quitted it. Archibald, I could not stay there. Had I done so, I should have been ill as you are. I think I should have died."

He said nothing for a few moments, and appeared to be lost in thought. Then he drew her face down to his, and kissed it.

"You ought not to have come over without my permission, Blanche."

"I did not travel alone. Mr. and Mrs. Arnold Ravensworth chanced to put up at the inn on their homeward route, and I took the opportunity to come over with them."

The information evidently did not please Lord Level. His brow contracted.

"You wrote me word that you had had an accident," she continued. "How could I be contented to remain away after that? So I came over: and I went to your rooms in Holles Street—"

"Why on earth did you go there?" he sharply interrupted. "When I had left them."

"But I did not know you had left them. How was I to know you had come to Marshdale if you never told me so? When I found you had left Holles Street, I went straight to Gloucester Place. Papa has just come home from Jersey."

"You ought to have remained in Germany until I was able to join you," he reiterated irritably; and Blanche could not avoid seeing that he was growing agitated and feverish. "What's to become of you? Where are you to be?"

"First of all, I want to have an explanation with you," said Blanche. "I came over on purpose to have it; to tell you many things. One is, that I will no longer submit to be treated as a child—"

"Blanche!" he curtly interrupted.

"Well?"

"You are acting as a child now, and as nothing else. This nonsense that you are talking—I am not in a condition to hear it."

"It is not nonsense," said Blanche.

"It is what I will not listen to. It was the height of folly to come here. All you can do now is to go back to London by the next train."

"Go back where?" she passionately asked. "I have no home in London."

"I dare say Major Carlen will receive you for a week. Before that time I hope to be well enough to come up, and prepare a home for you. Where are Sanders and Timms?"

"I did not bring them down with me. They are at an hotel. Why cannot I stay here?"

"Because I won't have it. There is nothing in the place ready for you, or suited to you."

"If it is suited to you, it's suited to me. I say I will not be treated as a child any longer. I could be quite happy here. There is nothing I should like so much as to explore this old house. I never saw such an array of ghostly passages anywhere."

Something in the words seemed dangerously to excite Lord Level. The fever was visibly increasing.

"I forbid you to explore; I forbid you to remain here!" he exclaimed in the deepest agitation. "Do you hear me, Blanche?—you must return by the next train."

"I will not," she replied, quite as obstinate as he. "I will not go hence until I have had an explanation with you. If you are too ill at present, I will wait for it."

He was, indeed, too ill. "Quiet, above all things," the doctor had said when he had paid his early morning visit. But quiet Lord Level had not had; his wife had put an end to that. His talk grew random, his mind wandering; a paroxysm of fever ensued. In terror Lady Level rang the bell.

Mrs. Edwards answered it. Blanche gazed at her with astonishment, scarcely recognising her. She had put on her gala dress of days long gone by: a short, full, red petticoat, a chintz gown looped above it in festoons, high-heeled shoes, buckles, snow-white stockings with worked "clocks," a mob cap of clear lace, large gold earrings, and black mittens. All this she had assumed out of respect to her new lady.

"Is he out of his mind?" gasped Lady Level, terrified at her lord's words and his restless motions.

"It is the fever, my lady," said Mrs. Edwards. "Dear, dear! And we thought him so much better today!"

Close upon that, Dr. Macferraty, the medical man, came in. He was of square-built frame with broad shoulders, very dictatorial and positive considering his years, which did not number more than seven-and-twenty.

"What mischief has been at work here?" he demanded, standing over the bed with Mrs. Edwards. "Who has been with him?"

She explained that Lady Level had arrived and had been talking with his lordship. She—Mrs. Edwards—had begged her ladyship *not* to talk to him; but—well, the young were heedless and did not think of consequences.

"If she has worried him into brain-fever, she will have herself to thank for it," harshly spoke the doctor. And Lady Level, who was in the adjoining room, overheard the words.

"Something has happened to agitate my patient!" exclaimed Doctor Macferraty, when, in leaving the room, he encountered Lady Level in the passage, and was introduced to her by Mrs. Edwards.

"I am very sorry," she answered. "We were speaking of family affairs, and Lord Level grew excited."

"Then, madam," said the doctor, "do not speak of family affairs again, whilst he is in this weak condition, or of any other affairs likely to excite him. You must, if you please, put off all such topics until he is better."

"How long will that be?" asked Lady Level.

"I cannot say; it may be a week, or it may be a month. When once these intermittent fevers get into the system, it is difficult to shake them off again."

"It will not go on to—to anything worse?" questioned Lady Level timidly, recalling what she had just overheard.

"I hope not; but I cannot answer for it. Your ladyship must be good enough to bear in mind that much depends upon his keeping himself tranquil, and upon those around helping to keep him so."

The doctor withdrew as he spoke, telling Mrs. Edwards that he would look in again at night. Lord Level remained very excited throughout the rest of the day; he had a bad night, the fever continuing, and was no better in the morning. Mrs. Edwards had sat up with him.

Lady Level then made up her mind to remain at Marshdale, consulting neither her lord nor anyone else. As Major Carlen had remarked, Blanche was developing a will of her own. Though, indeed, it might not have been right to leave him in his present condition. She sent for Sanders and Timms, the two servants who had attended her from Germany, and for certain luggage belonging to herself. Mrs. Edwards did the best she could with this influx of visitors to a scantily-furnished house. Lady Level occupied the chamber that opened from her husband's; it also opened on to the corridor.

"Madam," said Dr. Macferraty to her, taking the bull by the horns on one of the earliest days, "you must allow me to give you a word of advice. Do not, just at present, enter Lord Level's chamber; wait until he is a little stronger. He has just asked me whether you had gone back to town, and I did not say no. It is evident that your being here troubles him. The house, as it is at present, is not in a condition to receive you, or he appears to think so. Therefore, so long as he is in this precarious state, do not show yourself to him. Let him think you have returned to London."

"Is his mind quite right again?"

"By no means. But he has lucid intervals. I assure your ladyship it is of the very utmost importance that he should be kept tranquil. Otherwise, I will not answer for the consequences."

Lady Level took the advice in all humility. Bitterly though she was feeling upon some scores towards her husband, she did not want him to die; no, nor to have brain-fever. So she kept the door closed between her room and his, and was as quiet as a mouse at all times. And the days began to pass on.

Blanche found them monotonous. She explored the house, but the number of passages, short and long, their angles and their turnings, confused her. She made the acquaintance of the steward, Mr. Drewitt, an elderly gentleman who went about in a plum-coloured suit and a large cambric frill to his shirt. One autumn morning when Blanche had traversed the long corridor, beyond the rooms which she and Lord Level occupied, she turned into another at right angles with it, and came to a door that was partly open. Passing through it, she found herself in a narrow passage that she had not before seen. Deborah, the good-natured housemaid, suddenly came out of one of the rooms opening from it, carrying a brush and dustpan. Deborah was the only servant kept in the house, so far as Lady Level saw, apart from the cook, who was fat and experienced.

"What a curious old house!" exclaimed Lady Level. "Nothing but dark passages that turn and wind about until you don't know where you are."

"It is that, my lady," answered Deborah. "In the late lord's time the servants took to calling it the maze, it puzzled them so. The name got abroad, and some people call it the maze to this day."

"I don't think I have been in this passage before. Does anyone live or sleep here?" added Lady Level, looking at the household articles Deborah carried.

It was a dark, narrow passage, closed in by a door at each end. The door at the upper end was of oak; heavy, and studded with nails. Four rooms opened from the passage, two on each side.

"All these rooms are occupied by the master and missis," said Deborah, alluding to the steward and his sister. "This is Mrs. Edwards's chamber, my lady," pointing to the one she had just quitted. "That beyond it is Mr. Drewitt's; the opposite room is their sitting-room, and the one beside it is not used."

"Where does that heavy door lead to?" continued Lady Level.

"It leads into the East Wing, my lady," replied Deborah. "I have never entered that wing all the two years I've lived here," continued the gossiping girl. "I am not allowed to do so. The door is kept locked; as well as the door answering to it in the passage below."

"Does no one ever go into it?"

"Why, yes, my lady; Mr. Drewitt does, and spends a good part of his time there. He has a business-room there, in which he keeps his books and papers relating to the estate. Mrs. Edwards is in there, too, with him most days. And my lord goes in when he is down here."

"Then no one really inhabits that wing?"

"Oh yes, my lady, John Snow and his wife live in it; he's the head gardener. A many years he has been in the family; and one of the last things the late lord did before he died was to give him that wing to live in. An easy life Snow has of it now; working or not, just as he pleases. When there's any unusual work to be done, our gardener on this side is had in to help with it."

Lady Level did not feel much interested in the wing, or in Snow the gardener. But it happened that not half an hour after this conversation, she chanced to see Mrs. Snow.

Leaning, in her listlessness, out of an open window that was just above the side entrance, to which she had been conducted by the boy on her way from the station, she was noticing how high the wall was that separated the garden of the house from the garden of the East Wing. Lofty trees, closely planted, also flanked the wall, so that not the slightest glimpse could be had on either side of the other garden. The East Wing, with its grounds, was as completely hidden from view as though it had no existence. While rather wondering at this—for the East Wing was, after all, a part of the house, and not detached from it—Lady Level saw a woman emerge from a little sheltered doorway in the wall, lock it after her, and come up the path, key in hand. This obscure doorway, and another at the foot of the East Wing garden opening to the road, were apparently the only means of entrance to it. To the latter door, always kept locked, was attached a large bell, which awoke the surrounding echoes whenever tradespeople or other applicants rang at it.

"Is that you, Hannah Snow?" cried the cook, stepping forward to meet the other as she came up the path. "And how are you to-day? Do you want anything?"

Catching the name, Lady Level looked out more closely. She saw a tall, strong, respectable woman of middle age, with a smiling, happy face, and laughing hazel eyes. She wore a neat white cap, a clean cotton gown and gray-checked apron.

"Yes, cook," was the answer, given in a merry voice. "I want you to give me a handful of candied peel. I am preparing a batch of cakes for my old man, never supposing I had not all the ingredients at hand, and I find I have no peel. I'm sure I had some; and I tell John he must have stolen it."

"What a shame!" cried the cook, taking the words more literally than they were intended. Mrs. Snow laughed.

"Fact is, I suppose I used the last of it in the bread-and-butter pudding I made last week," said she.

"You are always making cakes for that man o' yours, seems to me, Hannah," grumbled the cook. "We can smell them over here when they're baking, and that's pretty often."

"Seems I am: he's always asking for them," assented Hannah. "He likes to eat one now and then between meals, you see.

"Well, he's a rare one for his inside," retorted the cook, as she went in for the candied peel.

"They seem to do very much as they like here," was the only thought that crossed Lady Level.

On this same day Lord Level, who had grown so much better as to be out of danger, dismissed his doctor. Presenting him with a handsome cheque, he told him that he required no further attendance. Blanche received the news from Mrs. Edwards.

"But is he so well as that?" she asked, in surprise.

"Well, my lady, he is very much better, there's no doubt of that. He will be out of bed to-morrow or the next day, and, if he takes care, will have no relapse," was the housekeeper's answer. "No doubt it might be safer for the doctor to continue to come a little longer, if it were only to enjoin strict quiet; but you see my lord does not like him."

"I fancied he did not."

"He is not our own doctor, as perhaps your ladyship has heard," pursued Mrs. Edwards. "*He* is a Mr. Hill: a clever, pleasant man, of a certain age, who was very intimate with the late lord. They were close friends, I may say. When his lordship met with this accident, it put him out uncommonly that we had to send for the young man, Dr. Macferraty, Mr. Hill being away."

"If Lord Level is so well as to do without a doctor, I might go into his room. Don't you think so, Mrs. Edwards?"

"Better not for a day or two, my lady; better not, indeed. I'm afraid my lord will be angry at your having stayed here—there being no fitting establishment or accommodation for your ladyship; and—"

"That is such nonsense!" interrupted Lady Level. "With Sanders and Timms here, I am more attended to than is really necessary. And even if I had to put up with discomfort for a short time, I dare say I should survive it."

"And it might cause his lordship excitement, I was about to say," quickly continued Mrs. Edwards. "A very little thing would bring the fever back again."

Blanche sighed rebelliously, but recognised the obligation to condemn herself a little longer to this dreary existence.

CHAPTER XI
THE QUARREL

THE following day was charmingly fine: the sun brilliant, the air warm as summer. In the afternoon Lady Level went out to take a walk. Lord Level was not up that day, but would be, all being well, on the morrow. It was the injury to the knee more than his general health that was keeping him in bed now.

Outside the gate Blanche looked about her, and decided to take the way towards the railway station. Upper Marshdale lay close beyond it, and she thought she would see what the little town was like. If she felt tired after exploring it, she could engage the solitary railway fly to bring her home again.

She went along the deserted road, passing a peasant's cottage now and then. Very near to the station she met the surly boy. He was coming along with a leap and a whistle, and stopped dead at sight of Lady Level.

"I say," said he, in a low tone, all his glee and his impudence gone out of him, "be you going *there*?"

"Yes," answered Lady Level, half smiling, for the boy amused her. He had pointed to indicate the station, but so awkwardly that she thought he pointed to the roofs and chimneys beyond it. "Yes, I am. Why?"

His face fell. "Not to tell of *me*?" he gasped.

"To tell of you! What should I have to tell of you?"

"About that there half-crown. You *give* him to me, mind; I never asked. You can't see the station-master if you try: he's a gone to his tea."

"Oh, I won't tell of that," said Lady Level. "I am going to the village, not to the station."

"They'd make such a row," said the boy, somewhat relieved. "The porter'd be mad that it wasn't given to him; he might get me sent away perhaps for't. It's such a lot, you see: a whole half-crown: when anything is given, it's a sixpence. But 'tain't nothing that's given mostly; *nothing*."

The intense resentment thrown into the last word made Lady Level laugh.

"It's a sight o' time, weeks and weeks, since I've had anything given me afore, barring the three penny pieces from Mr. Snow," went on the grumbling boy. "And what's three penny pieces?"

"Mr. Snow?" repeated Lady Level. "Who is he?"

"He is Lord Level's head gardener, he be. He comes up here to the station one day, not long afore you come down; and he collars the fly for the next down-train. The next down-train comes in and brings my lord and a lady with him. Mr. Snow, he puts the lady inside, and he puts what luggage there were outside. 'Twasn't much, and I helps him, and he dives into his pockets and brings out three penny pieces. And I'll swear that for weeks afore nobody had never given me a single farthing."

Lady Level changed colour. "What's your name?" she suddenly asked the boy, to cover her confusion.

"It be Sam Doughty. That there lady—"

"Oh, I know the lady," she carelessly interrupted, hating herself at the same time for pursuing the subject and the questions. "A lady with black hair and eyes, was it not, and long gold earrings?"

"Well, it were. I noticed the earrings, d'ye see, the sun made 'em sparkle so. Handsome earrings they was; as handsome as she were."

"And Lord Level took her home with him in the fly, did he?"

"That he didn't. She went along of herself, Mr. Snow a-riding on the box. My lord walked across the fields. The station-master telled him to mind the bull, but my lord called back that he warn't afraid."

There was nothing more to ask; nothing more that she could ask. But Lady Level had heard enough to disturb her equanimity, and she turned without going on to Upper Marshdale. That the lady with the gold earrings was either in the house, or in its East Wing, and that that was why she was wanted out of it, seemed clearer to her than the sun at noonday.

That same evening, Lady Level's servants were at supper in the large kitchen: where, as no establishment was kept up in the house, they condescended to take their meals. Deborah was partly waiting on them, partly gossiping, and partly dressing veal cutlets and bacon in the Dutch oven for what she called the upstairs supper. The cook had gone to bed early with a violent toothache.

"You have enough there, I hope," cried Timms, as Deborah brought the Dutch oven to the table to turn the cutlets.

"Old Mr. Drewitt has such an appetite; leastways at his supper," answered Deborah.

"I wonder they don't take their meals below; it's a long way to carry them up all them stairs," remarked Mr. Sanders, when Deborah was placing her dish of cutlets on the tray prepared for it.

"Oh, I don't mind it; I'm used to it now," said the good-humoured girl, as she went off with a quick step.

Deborah returned with a quieter step than she had departed. "They are quarrelling like anything!" she exclaimed in a low, frightened voice. "She's gone into my lord's room, and they are having it out over something or other."

Timms, who was then engaged in eating some favourite custard pudding, looked up. "What? Who? Do you mean my lord and my lady? How do you know, Deborah?"

"I heard them wrangling as I went by. I have to pass their rooms, you know, to get to Mr. Drewitt's rooms, and I heard them still louder as I came back. They are quarrelling just like common people. Has she a temper?"

"No," said Timms. "He has, though; that is, he can be frightfully passionate at times."

"He is not thought so in this house," returned Deborah. "To hear my master and mistress talk, my lord is just an angel upon earth."

"Ah!" said Timms, sniffing significantly.

Her supper ended, but not her curiosity, Timms stole a part of the way upstairs, and listened. But she only came in for the end of the dispute, as she related to Mr. Sanders on her return. Lady Level, after some final speech of bitter reproach, passed into her room and shut the door with a force that shook the walls, and probably shook Lord Level, who relieved his wrath by a little delicate language. So much Timms heard; but of what the quarrel had been about, she did not gather the faintest glimmer.

The house went to rest. Silence, probably sleep, had reigned within it for some two hours, and the clock had struck one, when wild calls of alarm, coupled with the ringing of his bell, issued from Lord Level's chamber. The servants rose hastily, in terror. Those cries of fear came not from their lord, but from Lady Level.

Sanders, partly attired, hastened thither; Timms, in a huge shawl, opened her door and stopped him; Deborah came flying down the long corridor. Mrs. Edwards was already in Lord Level's chamber. Lady Level, in a blue silk wrapping-gown, her cries of alarm over, lay panting in a chair, extremely agitated; and Lord Level was in a fainting-fit on his bed, with a stab in his arm, and another in his side, from which blood was flowing.

Some hours later, Mr. and Mrs. Arnold Ravensworth were at breakfast in Portland Place, when Major Carlen entered without ceremony. His purple-and-scarlet cloak, without which he rarely stirred out, had come unfastened and trailed behind him; his face looked scared and crestfallen.

"I must see you, I must see you!" cried the Major, throwing up his hands, as if apologizing for the intrusion. "It's on a matter of life and death."

"We have finished breakfast," said Mrs. Ravensworth; and she rose and left them together.

The Major strode up to Arnold, his teeth actually chattering. "I told you what it would be," he muttered. "I warned you of the consequences, if you helped Blanche to go down there. She has attempted his life."

Mr. Ravensworth gazed at him inquiringly.

"By George she has! They had a blowup last night, it seems, and she has stabbed him. It can be no one else who has done it. When these delicate girls are put up; made jealous, and that sort of thing; they are as bad as their more furious sisters. Witness that character of Scott's—what's her name?—Lucy, in the 'Bride of Lam—'"

"For pity's sake, Major Carlen, what are you saying?" interrupted Mr. Ravensworth, scarcely knowing whether the Major was mad or sane, or had been taking dinner in place of breakfast. "Don't introduce trashy romance into the woes of real life! Has anything happened at Lord Level's, or has it not?"

"He is stabbed, I tell you. One of Lord Level's servants, Sanders, arrived before I was up, with a note from Blanche. Here, read it!" But the Major's hand and the note shook together as he held it out.

> Do, dear papa, hasten down! A shocking event has happened to Lord Level. He has been stabbed in bed. I am terrified out of my senses.
>
> "Blanche Level."

"Now, she has done it," whispered the Major again, his stony eyes turned on Mr. Ravensworth in dread. "As sure as that her name's Blanche Level, it is she who has done it!"

"Nonsense! Impossible. Have you learnt any of the details?"

"A few scraps. As much as the man knew. He says they were awakened by cries in the middle of the night, and found Lord Level had been stabbed; and her ladyship was with him, screaming, and fainting on a chair. 'Who did it, Sanders?' said I. 'It's impossible to make out who did it, sir,' said he; 'there was no one indoors to do it, and all the house was in bed.' 'What do the police say?' I asked. 'The police are not called in, sir,' returned he; 'my lord and my lady won't have it done.' Now, Ravensworth, what can be clearer proof than that? I used to think her mother had a tendency to insanity; I did, by Jove! she went once or twice into such a tantrum with me. Though she had a soft, sweet temper in general, mild as milk."

"Well, you must go down without delay.'

The grim old fellow put up his hands, which were trembling visibly. "I wouldn't go down if you gave me a hundred pounds a mile, poor as I am, just now. Look what a state I'm in, as it is: I had to get Sanders to hook my cloak for me, and he didn't half do it. I wouldn't interfere between Blanche and Level for a gold-mine. You must go down for me; I came to ask you to do so."

"It is impossible for me to go down today. I wish I knew more. How did you hear there had been any disagreement between them?"

"Sanders let it out. He said the women-servants heard Level and his wife hotly disputing."

"Where is Sanders?"

"In your hall. I brought him round with me."

The man was called in, and was desired to repeat what he knew of the affair. It was not much, and it has been already stated.

"Someone must have got in, Sanders," observed Mr. Ravensworth, when he had listened.

"Well, sir, I don't know," was the answer. "The curious thing is that there are no signs of it. All the doors and windows had been fastened before we went to bed, and they had not been, so far as we can discover, in the least disturbed."

"Do you suspect anyone in the house?"

"Why—no, sir; there's no one we like to suspect," returned Sanders, coughing dubiously.

"The servants—"

"Oh, none of the servants would do such a thing," interrupted Sanders, very decidedly: and Mr. Ravensworth feared they might be getting upon dangerous ground. He caught Major Carlen's significant glance. It said, as plainly as glance ever yet spoke, "The man suspects his mistress."

"Is Lord Level's bedroom isolated from the rest of the rooms?"

"Pretty well, sir, for that. No one sleeps near him but my lady. Her room opens from his."

"Could he have done it himself, Sanders?" struck in Major Carlen. "He has been light-headed from fever."

"Just at the first moment the same question occurred to me, sir; but we soon saw that it was not at all likely. The fever had abated, my lord was quite collected, and the stab in the arm could not have been done by himself."

"Was any instrument found?"

"Yes, sir: a clasp-knife, with a small, sharp blade. It was found on the floor of my lady's room."

An ominous silence ensued.

"Are the stabs dangerous?" inquired Mr. Ravensworth.

"It is thought they are only slight, sir. The danger will be if they bring back the fever. His lordship will not have a doctor called in—"

"Not have a doctor called in!"

"He forbids it absolutely, sir. When we reached his room, in answer to my lady's cries, he had fainted; but he soon recovered, and hearing Mrs. Edwards speak of the doctor, he refused to have him sent for."

"You ought to have sent, all the same," imperiously spoke Mr. Ravensworth.

Sanders smiled. "Ah, sir, but my lord's will is law."

Mr. Ravensworth turned to a side-table. He wrote a rapid word to Lady Level, promising to be with her that evening, gave it to Sanders, and bade him make the best of his way back to Marshdale. Certain business of importance was detaining him in town for the day.

"When you get down there, Ravensworth, you won't say that I wouldn't go, you know," said the Major. "Say I couldn't."

"What excuse can I make for you?"

"Any excuse that comes uppermost. Say I'm in bed with gout. I have charged Sanders to hold his tongue."

The day had quite passed before Mr. Ravensworth was able to start on his journey. It was dark when he reached Upper Marshdale. There he found Sanders and the solitary fly.

"Is Lord Level better?" was his first question.

"A little better this evening, sir, I believe; but he has again been off his head with fever, and Dr. Macferraty had, after all, to be called in," replied the man. "My lady is pretty nearly beside herself too."

"Have the police been called in yet?"

"No, sir; no chance of it; my lord and my lady won't have it done."

"It appears to be an old-fashioned place, Sanders," remarked Mr. Ravensworth, when they had reached the house.

"It's the most awkward turn-about place inside, sir, you ever saw; nothing but passages. But my lord never lives here; he only pays it promiscuous visits now and then, and brings down no servants with him. He was kept prisoner here, as may be said, through jamming his knee in a gateway; and then my lady came down, and we are putting up with all sorts of inconveniences."

"Who lives here in general?"

"Two old retainers of the Level family, sir: both of 'em sights to look upon; she especially. She dresses up like an old picture."

Waiting within the doorway to receive Mr. Ravensworth was Mrs. Edwards. He could not take his eyes from her. He had never seen one like her in real life, and Sanders's words, "dresses up like an old picture," recurred to him. He had thought this style of dress completely gone out of date, *except* in pictures; and here it was before him, worn by a living woman! She dropped him a stately curtsey, that would have served for the prelude to a Court minuet in the palmy days of Queen Charlotte.

"Sir, you are the gentleman expected by my lady?"

"Yes—Mr. Ravensworth."

"I'll show you in myself, sir."

Taking up a candle from a marble slab—there was no other light to be seen—she conducted him through the passage, and, turning down another which stood at right angles with it, halted at the door of a room. In answer to a question from Mr. Ravensworth, she said his lordship was much better within the last hour—quite himself again. "What would you be pleased to take, sir?" she added. "I will order it to be brought in to you."

"I require nothing, thank you."

But quite a housekeeper of the old school, and essentially hospitable, she would not take a refusal. "I hope you will, sir: tea—or coffee—or supper—?"

"A little coffee, then."

She dropped another of her ceremonious curtseys, and threw open the door. "The gentleman you expected, my lady."

It was another long, bare room, but not the one already mentioned. Singularly bare and empty it looked to-night. A large fire burned in the grate, halfway down the room, and in an easy-chair before it reclined Lady Level—asleep. Two wax-candles stood on the high carved mantelpiece, and the large oak table behind Lady Level was dark with age. Everything about the room was dreary, excepting the fire, the lights, and the sleeper.

Should he awaken her? He looked at Blanche Level and deliberated. Her feet rested on a footstool, and her head lay on the low back of the chair, a cushion under it. She wore an evening dress of light silk, trimmed with white lace. Her neck and arms, only relieved by the lace, looked cold and bare in the dreary room, for she wore no ornaments; nothing of gold or silver was about her—except her wedding-ring. Was it possible that she had attempted the life of him who had put on that ring? There was a careworn look on her face as she slept, which lessened her beauty, and two indented lines rose in her forehead, not usual to a girl of twenty; her mouth, slightly open, showed her teeth; and very pretty teeth were Lady Level's. No, thought Mr. Ravensworth, guilty of that crime she never had been!

Should he arouse her? A coal fell on to the hearth with a rattle, and settled the question, for Lady Level opened her eyes. A moment's dreamy unconsciousness, and then she started up, her face flushing.

"Oh, Arnold, I beg your pardon! I must have dropped asleep. How good of you to come!"

With a burst of tears she held out her hands; it seemed so glad a relief to have a friend there.

"Arnold, I am so miserable—so frightened! Why did not papa come down this morning?"

"He was—" Mr. Ravensworth searched for an excuse and did not find one easily "Something kept him in town, and he requested me to come down in his stead, and see if I could be of any use to you."

"Have you heard much about it?" she asked, in a whisper.

"Sanders told me and your father what little he knew. But it appeared most extraordinary to both of us. Sit down, Lady Level," he continued, drawing a chair nearer to hers. "You look ill and fatigued."

"I am not ill; unless uncertainty and anxiety can be called illness. Have you dined?"

"Yes; but your housekeeper insists on hospitality, and will send me up some coffee."

"Did you ever see so complete a picture as she is? Just like those engravings we admire in the old frames."

"Will you describe to me this—the details of the business I came down to hear?"

"I am trying to delay it," she said, with a forced laugh—a laugh that caused Mr. Ravensworth involuntarily to knit his brow, for it spoke of insincerity. "I think I will not tell you anything about it until to-morrow morning."

"I must leave again to-night. The last up-train passes—"

"Oh, but you will stay all night," she interrupted nervously. "I cannot be left alone. Mrs. Edwards is preparing a room for you somewhere."

"Well, we will discuss that by-and-by. What is this unpleasant business about Lord Level?"

"I don't know what it is," she replied. "He has been attacked and stabbed. I only know that it nearly frightened me to death."

"By whom was it done?"

"I don't know," she repeated. "They say the doors and windows were all fastened, and that no one could have got in."

Now, strange as it may appear, and firmly impressed as Mr. Ravensworth was with the innocence of Lady Level, there was a tone in her voice, a look in her countenance, as she spoke the last few sentences, that he did not like. Her manner was evasive, and she did not meet his glance openly.

"Were you in his room when it happened?"

"Oh dear no! Since I came down here I have occupied a room next to his; his dressing-room, I believe, when he stays here at ordinary times; and I was in bed and asleep at the time."

"Asleep?"

"Fast asleep. Until something woke me: and when I entered Lord Level's room, I found—I found—what had happened."

"Had it just happened?"

"Just. I was terrified. After I had called the servants, I think I nearly fainted. Lord Level quite fainted."

"But did you not see anyone in the room who could have attacked him?"

She shook her head.

"Nor hear any noise?"

"I—thought I heard a noise; I am positive I thought so. And I heard Lord Level's voice."

"That you naturally would hear. A man whose life is being attempted would not be likely to remain silent. But you must try and give me a better explanation than this. You say something suddenly awoke you. What was it?"

"I cannot tell you," repeated Lady Level.

"Was it a noise?"

"N—o; not exactly. I cannot say precisely what it was."

Mr. Ravensworth deliberated before he spoke again. "My dear Lady Level, this will not do. If these questions are painful to you, if you prefer not to trust me, they shall cease, and I will return to town as wise as I came, without having been able to afford you any assistance or advice. I think you could tell me more, if you would do so."

Lady Level burst into tears and grew agitated. A disagreeable doubt—guilty or not guilty?—stole over Mr. Ravensworth. "Oh, heaven, that it should be so!" he cried to himself, recalling how good and gentle she had been through her innocent girlhood. "I came down, hoping to be to you a true friend," he resumed in a low tone. "If you will allow me to be so, if you will confide in me, Blanche, come what may, I will stand by you."

There was a long silence. Mr. Ravensworth did not choose to break it. He had said his say, and the rest remained with Lady Level.

"Lord Level has made me very angry indeed," she broke out, indignation arresting her tears. "He has made me—almost—hate him."

"But you are not telling me what occurred."

"I have told you," she answered. "I was suddenly aroused from sleep, and then I heard Lord Level's voice, calling 'Blanche! Blanche!' I went into his room, ran up to him, and he put out his arms and caught me to him. Then I saw blood upon his nightshirt, and he told me he had been stabbed.

Oh, how I shuddered! I cannot think of it now without feeling sick and ill, without almost fainting," she added, a shiver running through her frame.

Mr. Ravensworth's opinion veered round again. "She do it—nonsense!" Lady Level continued:

"'Don't scream; don't scream, Blanche,' he said. 'I am not much hurt, and I will take care of you,' and he held me to him as though I were in a vice. I thought he did not want me to alarm the house."

"Did he keep you there long?"

"It seemed long to me: I don't suppose it was more than a couple of minutes. His hold gradually relaxed, and then I saw that he had fainted. Oh, the terror of that moment! all the more intense that it had been suppressed. I feared he might bleed to death. I opened the door, and cried and screamed, and called for the servants; I rushed back to the room and rang the bell; and then I fell back in the easy-chair, and could do no more."

"Well, this is a better explanation than you gave me at first," said Mr. Ravensworth encouragingly: and she had spoken more readily, without appearance of disguise. "Then it was Lord Level's calling to you that first aroused you?"

"No; oh no; it was not that. It—" she stopped in confusion. "At least—perhaps it was. It—I can't say." She had relapsed into evasion again, and once more Mr. Ravensworth was plunged in doubt. He leaned towards her.

"I am going to ask you a question, Lady Level, and you must of course answer it or not as you please. I can only repeat that any confidence you repose in me shall never be betrayed. Did Lord Level inflict this injury on himself?"

"No, that was impossible," she freely answered; "it must have been done to him."

"The weapon, I hear, was found in your room."

"Yes."

"But how could it have come there?"

"As if I knew!"

"Why do you object to the police being called in?"

"It was Lord Level who objected. When he recovered from his faintness, and heard them speaking of the police, he called Mr. Drewitt to him—who is master of the house under Lord Level—and charged him that nothing of the kind should be done. I would rather they were here," she added after a pause. "I should feel safer. This morning I went to my husband and told him if he would not have in the police, the house searched, and the facts investigated, I should die with terror. He replied, jestingly, then if I chose to be so foolish, I must die: the hurt was his, not mine, and if he saw no occasion for having in the police, and did not choose to have them in, surely I need not want them. I was perfectly safe, and so was he, he continued, and he would see that I was kept so. He would not even have the doctor called in at first; but towards midday, when the fever returned and he became delirious, Mr. Drewitt sent for him."

"That seems more strange than all—refusing to have a doctor. He—"

The arrival of coffee interrupted them. Sanders brought it in in a silver coffeepot on a silver tray, with biscuits and other light refreshments; and Mrs. Edwards attended to pour it out. Mr. Ravensworth repeated to her what he had just said about the doctor.

"The fact is, sir, my lord does not like Dr. Macferraty," she rejoined. "None of us in this house do like him; we cannot endure him. He has not long been in practice, and we look upon him as an upstart. It is a great misfortune that Mr. Hill is away just now."

"The usual attendant, I presume, Mrs. Edwards?"

"Yes, sir; and a friend besides. He and the late lord seemed almost like brothers, so intimate were they. Mr. Hill's mother is going on for ninety; she is beginning to break, and he has gone over to see her. She lives in the Isle of Man. It is almost a month since he went away."

"The late lord? Let me see. He was the present lord's uncle, was he not?"

"Why, no, sir; he was his father," returned Mrs. Edwards, surprised at the mistake. "The late peer, Archibald Lord Level, had two sons, Mr. Francis the heir, and Mr. Archibald. Mr. Francis died of consumption, and lies buried in the family vault in Marshdale Church; and Mr. Archibald, the only son left, succeeded to his father."

"Yes, yes, I had forgotten," said Mr. Ravensworth. "An idea was floating in my mind that the present peer had not been always the heir-apparent."

CHAPTER XII
MYSTERY

SILENCE had fallen upon the room. Coffee had been taken, and the tray carried away by Mrs. Edwards. It was yet only eight o'clock. Mr. Ravensworth sat in mental perplexity, believing he had not come to the bottom of this dreadful affair; no, nor half-way to it.

But Lady Level was in still greater perplexity, her mind buried in miserable reverie. A conviction that she was being frightfully wronged in some way, and that she would not bear it, lay uppermost with her. Since meeting with the railway boy, Sam Doughty, the previous afternoon, and hearing the curious information he had disclosed, her temper had been gradually rising. It was temper that had caused her to declare herself to Lord Level while the servants (as related in a former chapter) were at supper in the kitchen, and Mrs. Edwards and the old steward were shut up in their sitting-room, waiting for their own supper to be served. The coast thus clear, in went Blanche to her lord's chamber. Not to open out the budget of her wrongs—he might not be sufficiently well for that—but to announce herself. To let him see that she was still in the house, that she had disregarded his injunction to quit it; and to assure him, in her rebellious spirit, that she meant to remain in it as long as she pleased. Not a word of suspected and unorthodox matters did Lady Level breathe, and the quarrel that arose between them was wholly on the score of her disobedience. Lord Level was passionately angry, thus to have been set at naught. He told her that as his wife she owed him obedience, and must give it to him. She retorted that she would not do so. The dispute went no further than that; but loud and angry words passed on both sides. And the next episode in the drama, some three or four hours later, was the mysterious attack upon Lord Level.

"Arnold," suddenly spoke her ladyship, looking up from her chair, "I mean to take a very decisive step."

"In what way?" he quietly asked, from his seat on the other side of the fireplace. "To send for the police?"

"No, no, no; not that. I shall separate from Lord Level."

"Oh," said Mr. Ravensworth, taken by surprise, and thinking she was jesting.

"As soon as he is well again, and able to discuss matters, I shall demand a separation. I shall *insist* upon it. If he will not accord it to me privately, I shall apply for it publicly."

"Blanche, you will do no such thing!" he exclaimed, rising in excitement. "You do not know what you are saying."

"And you do not know how much cause I have for saying it," she answered. "Lord Level has—has—insulted me."

"Hush," said Mr. Ravensworth. "I don't quite know what you mean by insult—"

"And I cannot tell you," she interrupted, her pretty black satin slipper beating its indignation on the hearthrug, her cheeks wearing a delicate rose-flush. "It is a thing I can speak of only to himself."

"But—I was going to say—Lord Level does not, I feel sure, intrude personal insult upon you. Anything that may take place outside your knowledge you had better neither notice nor inquire into."

Lady Level shook her head defiantly. "I mean to do it."

"I will not hear another word upon this point," said Mr. Ravensworth sternly. "You are as yet not much more than a child, young lady; when you are a little older and wiser, you will see how foolish such ideas are. For your own sake, Blanche, put them away from you."

"I wish my dear brother Tom were here!" she petulantly returned. "It was a shame his regiment should be sent out to India!"

Mr. Ravensworth drew in his stern lips. He had suspected that of the dreadful fate of Tom Heriot she must still be ignorant. The suspicion was now confirmed.

At that moment the steward, Mr. Drewitt, appeared; and Lady Level introduced him by name. Mr. Ravensworth saw a pale, venerable man of sixty years, still strong and upright, looking like a gentleman of the old, old school, in his plum-coloured suit and white silk stockings, his silver knee-buckles, his low shoes, and his voluminous cambric shirt-frill. He brought a message from his lord, who wished to see Mr. Ravensworth.

"Who told his lordship that Mr. Ravensworth was here?" exclaimed Lady Level quickly.

"Madam, it was I. My lord heard someone being shown in to your ladyship, and inquired who had come. I am sorry he has asked for you, sir," candidly added the steward, as they left the room together. "The fever has abated, but the least excitement will bring it on again."

Lady Level was sorry also. She did not care that Mr. Ravensworth's presence in the house should be known upstairs. The fact was that one day when she and her husband were on their homeward journey from Savoy, and Blanche was indulging in odds and ends of grievances against her lord, as in her ill-feeling towards him she was then taking to do, she had spoken a few words in sheer perverseness of spirit to make him jealous of Arnold Ravensworth. Lord Level said nothing, but he took the words to heart. He had not liked that gentleman before; he hated him now. Blanche blushed for herself as she recalled it.

Of course, it was not the visitor likely to give most pleasure to Lord Level. As the steward introduced Mr. Ravensworth and left them together, Lord Level regarded him with a cold, stern glance.

"So it is you!" he exclaimed. "May I ask what brings you down here? Did my lady send for you?"

"No," answered Mr. Ravensworth, advancing towards the bed. "Major Carlen called at my house this morning and requested me to come down. I could not reach Marshdale before to-night."

"Major Carlen? Oh! very good. Major Carlen dare not interfere between me and my wife; and he knows that."

"So far as I believe, Major Carlen has no intention or wish to interfere. Lady Level sent to him in her alarm, and he requested me to come down in his place."

"If Major Carlen has entered into an arrangement with you to come to my house and pry into matters that concern myself alone—"

"I beg your lordship's pardon," was the curt interruption. "I do not like or respect Major Carlen sufficiently well to enter into any 'arrangement' with him. I came down here, certainly in compliance with his desire, but in a spirit of kindness towards Lady Level, and to be of assistance to yourself if it were possible."

"How came you to bring Lady Level over from Germany?"

"She wished to come over."

"And I wished and desired her to stay there until I could join her. Do you call *that* interference?"

"It was nothing of the kind. On the morning of our departure from the inn, Lady Level told my wife and myself that she should take the opportunity to travel with us. She and her servants were even then dressed for the journey, and her travelling-carriage stood ready packed in the yard. If she did this against your wish, I am in no way responsible for it. It was not my place to dictate to her; to say she should go, or should remain. Be assured, my lord, I am the last man in the world unduly to interfere with other people; and my coming down now was entirely brought about by Major Carlen."

Lord Level was not insensible to reason. He remained silent for a time, the angry expression gradually leaving his face. Mr. Ravensworth spoke:

"I hope this injury to your lordship will not prove a grave one."

"It is a trifle," was the answer; "nothing but a trifle. It is my knee that keeps me prostrate here more than anything else; and I have intermittent fever with it."

"Can I be of service to you? If so, command me."

"Much obliged. No, I do not want anyone to be of service to me, if you allude to this stabbing business. Some drunken fellow got in, and—"

"The servants say the doors were all left fastened, and were so found."

"The servants say so to conceal their carelessness," cried Lord Level, as a contortion of pain crossed his face. "This knee gives me twinges at times like a red-hot iron."

"If anyone had broken in, especially any—"

"Mr. Ravensworth," imperatively interrupted Lord Level, "it is my pleasure that this affair should not be investigated. I say that some man got in—a poacher, probably, who must have been the worse for drink—and he attacked me, not knowing what he was doing. To have a commotion made over it would only excite me in my present feverish condition. Therefore I shall put up with the injury, and shall be well all the sooner for doing so. You will be so obliging," he added, some sarcasm in his tone, "as to do the same."

But now, Mr. Ravensworth did not show himself wise in that moment. He urged, in all good faith, a different course upon his lordship. The presumption angered and excited Lord Level. In no time, as it seemed, and without sufficient cause, the fever returned and mounted to the brain. His face grew crimson, his eye wild; his voice rose almost to a scream, and he flung his uninjured arm about the bed. Mr. Ravensworth, in self-reproach for what he had done, looked for the bell and rang it.

"Drewitt, are the doors fastened?" raved his lordship in delirium, as the steward hastened in. "Do you hear me, Drewitt? Have you looked to the doors? You must have left one of them open! Where are the keys? The keys, I say, Drewitt!—What brings that man here?"

"You had better go down, sir, out of his sight," whispered the steward, for it was at Mr. Ravensworth the invalid was excitedly pointing. "I knew what it would be if he began talking. And he was so much better!"

"His lordship excites himself for nothing," was the deprecating answer.

"Why, of course," said Mr. Drewitt. "It is the nature of fever-patients to do so."

Mrs. Edwards came in with appliances to cool the heated head, and Mr. Ravensworth returned to the sitting-room below. Blanche was not there. Close upon that, Dr. Macferraty called. After he had been with his patient and dressed the wounds, he came bustling into the sitting-room. This loud young man had a nose that turned straight up, giving an impudent look to the face, and wide-open, round green eyes. But no doubt he had his good points, and was a skilful surgeon.

"You are a friend of the family, I hear, sir," he began. "I hope you intend to order an investigation into this extraordinary affair?"

"I have no authority for doing so. And Lord Level does not wish it done."

"A fig for Lord Level! He does not know what he's saying," cried Dr. Macferraty. "There never was so monstrous a thing heard of as that a nobleman should be stabbed in his own bed and the assassin be let off scot-free! We need not look far for the culprit!"

The last words, significantly spoken, jarred on Mr. Ravensworth's ears. "Have you a suspicion?" he asked.

"I can put two and two together, sir, and find they make four. The windows were fast; the doors were fast; there was no noise, no disturbance, no robbery: well, then, what deduction have we to fall back upon but that the villain, he or she, is an inmate of the house?"

Mr. Ravensworth's pulses beat a shade more quickly. "Do you suspect one of the servants?"

"Yes, I do."

"But the servants are faithful and respectable. They are not suspected indoors, I assure you."

"Perhaps not; they are out-of-doors, though. The whole neighbourhood is in commotion over it; and how Drewitt and the old lady can let these two London servants be at large is the talk of the place."

"Oh, it is the London servants you suspect, then, or one of them?"

"Look here," said Dr. Macferraty, dropping his voice and bending forward in his chair till his face almost touched Mr. Ravensworth's: "that the deed was done by an inmate of the house is *certain*. No one got in, or could have got in; it is nonsense to suggest it. The inmates consist of Lady Level and the servants only. If you take it from the servants, you must lay it upon her."

No answer.

"Well," went on the doctor, "it is impossible to suspect *her*. A delicate, refined girl, as she is, could not do so evil a thing. So we must needs look to the servants. Deborah would not do it; the stout old cook could not. She was in bed ill, besides, and slept through all the noise and confusion. The two other servants, Sanders and Timms, are strangers."

"I feel sure they no more did it than I," impulsively spoke Mr. Ravensworth.

"Then you would fall back upon Lady Level?"

"No. No," flashed Mr. Ravensworth. "The bare suggestion of the idea is an insult to her."

Dr. Macferraty drew himself back in his chair. "There's a mystery in the affair, look at it which way you will, sir," he cried raspingly. "My lord says he did not recognise the assassin; but, if he did not, why should he forbid investigation? Put it as you do, that the two servants are innocent—why, then, I fairly own I am puzzled. Another thing puzzles me: the knife was found in Lady Level's chamber, yet she protests that she slept through it all—was only awakened by his lordship calling to her when it was over."

"It may have been flung in."

"No; it was carried in; for blood had dripped from it all along the floor."

"Has the weapon been recognised?"

"Not that I am aware of. No one owns to knowing it. Anyway, it is an affair that ought to be, and that must be, inquired into officially," concluded the doctor from the corridor, as he said good-night and went bustling out.

Mr. Ravensworth, standing at the sitting-room door, saw him meet the steward, who must have overheard the words, and now advanced with cautious steps. Touching Mr. Ravensworth's arm, he drew him within the shadow cast by a remote corner.

"Sir," he whispered, "my lady told Mrs. Edwards that you were a firm friend of hers; a sure friend?"

"I trust I am, Mr. Drewitt."

"Then let it drop, sir; it is no common robber who has done this. Let it drop, for her sake and my lord's."

Mr. Ravensworth felt painfully perplexed. Those few words, spoken by the faithful old steward, were more fraught with suspicion against Lady Level than anything he had yet heard.

Returning to the sitting-room, pacing it to and fro in his perplexity for he knew not how long, he was looking at his watch to ascertain the time, when Lady Level came in. She had been in Lord Level's sitting-room upstairs, she said, the one opposite his bed-chamber. He was somewhat calmer now. Mr. Ravensworth thought that he must now be going.

"I have been of no assistance to you, Lady Level; I do not see that I can be of any," he observed. "But should anything arise in which you think I can help you, send for me."

"What do you expect to arise?" she hastily inquired.

"Nay, I expect nothing."

"Did Lord—" Lady Level suddenly stopped and turned her head. Just within the room stood two policemen. She rose with a startled movement, and shrank close to Mr. Ravensworth, crying out, as for protection. "Arnold! Arnold!"

"Do not agitate yourself," he whispered. "What is it that you want?" he demanded, moving towards the men.

"We have come about this attack on Lord Level, sir," replied one of them.

"Who sent for you?"

"Don't know anything about that, sir. Our superior ordered us here, and is coming on himself. We must examine the fastenings of this window, sir, by the lady's leave."

They passed up the room, and Lady Level left it, followed by Mr. Ravensworth. Outside stood Deborah, aghast.

"They have been in the kitchen this ten minutes, my lady," she whispered, "asking questions of us all—Mr. Sanders and Mrs. Timms and me and cook, all separate. And now they are going round the house to search it, and see to the fastenings."

The men came out again and moved away, Deborah following slowly in their wake: she appeared to regard them with somewhat of the curiosity we give to a wild animal: but Mr. Ravensworth recalled her. Lady Level entered the room again and sat down by the fire. Mr. Ravensworth again observed that he must be going: he had barely time to walk to the station and catch the train.

"Arnold, if you go, and leave me with these men in the house, I will never forgive it!" she passionately uttered.

He looked at her in surprise. "I thought you wished for the presence of the police. You said you should regard them as a protection."

"Did *you* send for them?" she breathlessly exclaimed.

"Certainly not."

She sank into a reverie—a deep, unpleasant reverie that compressed her lips and contracted her brow. Suddenly she lifted her head.

"He is my husband, after all, Arnold."

"To be sure he is."

"And therefore—and therefore—there had better be no investigation."

"Why?" asked Mr. Ravensworth, scarcely above his breath.

"Because he does not wish it," she answered, bending her face downwards. "He forbade me to call in aid, or to suffer it to be called in; and, as I say, he is my husband. Will you stop those men in their search? will you send them away?"

"I do not think I have power to do so."

"You can forbid them in Lord Level's name. I give you full authority: as he would do, were he capable of acting. Arnold, I *will* have them out of the house. I *will*."

"What is it that you fear from them?"

"I fear—I cannot tell you what I fear. They might question me."

"And if they did?—you can only repeat to them what you told me."

"No, it must not be," she shivered. "I—I—dare not let it be."

Mr. Ravensworth paused. "Blanche," he said, in low tones, "have you told me all?"

"Perhaps not," she slowly answered.

"'Perhaps!'"

"There!" she exclaimed, springing up in wild excitement. "I hear those men upstairs, and you stand here idly talking! Order them away in Lord Level's name."

Desperately perplexed, Mr. Ravensworth flew to the stairs. The steward, pale and agitated, met him half-way up. "It must not be looked into by the police," he whispered. "Sir, it must not. Will you speak to them? you may have more weight with them than I. Say you are a friend of my lord's. I strongly suspect this is the work of that meddling Macferraty."

Arnold Ravensworth moved forward as one in a dream, an under-current of thought asking what all this mystery meant. The steward followed. They found the men in one of the first rooms: not engaged in the examination of its fastenings or its closets (and the whole house abounded in closets and cupboards), but with their heads together, talking in whispers.

In answer to Mr. Ravensworth's peremptory demand, made in Lord Level's name, that the search should cease and the house be freed of their presence, they civilly replied that they must not leave, but would willingly retire to the kitchen and there await their superior officer, who was on his road to the house: and they went down accordingly. Mr. Ravensworth returned to the sitting-room to acquaint Lady Level with the fact, but found she had disappeared. In a moment she came in, scared, her hands lifted in dismay, her breath coming in gasps.

"Give me air!" she cried, rushing to the window and motioning to have it opened. "I shall faint; I shall die."

"What ever is the matter?" questioned Mr. Ravensworth, as he succeeded in undoing the bolt of the window, and throwing up its middle compartment. At that moment a loud ring came to the outer gate. It increased her terror, and she broke into a flood of tears.

"My dear young lady, let me be your friend," he said in his grave concern. "Tell me the whole truth. I know you have not done so yet. Let it be what it will, I promise to—if possible—shield you from harm."

"Those men are saying in the kitchen that it was I who attacked Lord Level; I overheard them," she shuddered, the words coming from her brokenly in her agitation.

"Make a friend of me; you shall never have a truer," he continued, for really he knew not what else to urge, and he could not work in the dark. "Tell me all from beginning to end."

But she only shivered in silence.

"Blanche!—did—you—do—it?"

"No," she answered, with a low burst of heartrending sobs. "*But I saw it done.*"